ABOUT THE AUTHOR

Anthony Irvin studied veterinary medicine at Cambridge University, and after a period in UK farming practice, went to East Africa for two years and stayed for twenty where he became an expert on a disease of cattle and wildlife that no one outside Africa has ever heard of. During this time he travelled widely through the region and worked closely with indigenous people such as the Maasai.

He has camped amongst elephants, canoed amongst hippos, windsurfed amongst stingrays, climbed Africa's highest mountain, eaten crocodile and photographed a rhino in his pyjamas. He is happiest when driving his Land Rover through the bush or eating haggis by an African campfire.

He now lives in wild Suffolk with his wife, two children and a collection of other animals, including a Parson Russell terrier called Tigger. The closest he gets to an off-road vehicle these days is a ride-on mower, but when the opportunity arises, he returns to the tropics to refuel his passion for hot places and their wildlife.

To Jack and Ollie

THE ANT-LION
An African Safari Adventure

Karibuni Afrika

Anthony Irvin

Anthony Irvin

Illustrations by Cat Sawyer
Cover Design by Catherine Duncumb

Matador
5 Weir Road
Kibworth Beauchamp
Leicester LE8 0LQ, UK
Tel: (+44) 116 279 2299
Email: books@troubador.co.uk
Web: www.troubador.co.uk/matador

ISBN 9781848762077

A Cataloguing-in-Publication (CIP) catalogue record for this book
is available from the British Library.

Printed in the UK by TJ International, Padstow, Cornwall

Matador is an imprint of Troubador Publishing Ltd

For REBECCA who liked feeding the giraffes,
and JOSH who wanted to see an aardvark in the wild.

ACKNOWLEDGEMENTS

While living and working in East Africa, I spent many weeks on safari and nights camping in the bush. My grateful thanks to those knowledgeable people who shared that passion, and from whom I learned so much about Africa, its remote places, its people and its spectacular wildlife, in particular: Ken Bock, Simon Evans, Michael Gwynne, Lionel Hartley, Robin Newson, Peter Stevenson; and to Bajila and Shillingi for showing me something of their bush craft. I am especially grateful to Sarah Such for her wise counsel, and for her literary and editorial advice; and my grateful thanks to colleagues who read and commented on numerous drafts and rewrites, particularly: Valerie and David Axton, Carolyn Belcher, Claire Frank, Ann Jessett, Sue Sawyer and George Wicker. Many thanks also to Olivia Wicker, my junior reader, and to Nick Heard, who introduced me to flying light aircraft. My grateful thanks to Cat Sawyer and Catherine Duncumb who have applied their complementary artistic skills in portraying Africa and its animals so evocatively. I am most grateful to my family, Susanna, Rebecca and Josh for their patience and forbearance while I was incarcerated behind closed doors, and for coming to the rescue with perceptive thoughts and ideas at key moments. My final thanks are to Jeremy Thompson and all at Matador for being so supportive, and for making the publication process not only painless but also pleasurable.

FOREWORD

The Ant-Lion conjures up the sights, smells and sounds of East Africa and is sure to give young readers a superb introduction to the myriad beauties, wonders, problems, cultures and wildlife of this remarkable region.

Drawn from the author's decades of experience travelling the dusty roads of Africa, the book displays a fantastic quirky curiosity about creatures great and small, all beautifully illustrated. Such accounts of the wildlife really capture the imagination and feed the terrific spirit of adventure the book conveys.

Whilst the author doesn't duck the all-too-common problems of East Africa, *The Ant-Lion* leaves the reader with a profound feeling of optimism and love for the place. *The Ant-Lion* will make many youngsters wish they were living under African skies with Fupi and friends.

Matt Fletcher
Author of Lonely Planet's Guides on
East Africa and *Trekking in East Africa*

MAP OF TANZANIA

Showing main towns and features, and presumed location of Simba Ranch.

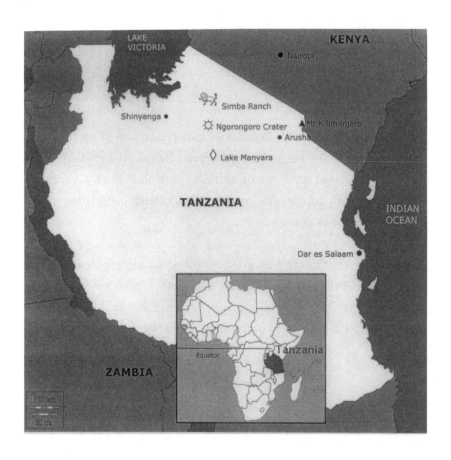

CHAPTER 1

Fupi

TROUBLE AT THE RANCH

A cartoon rat peered at Lucy from the cereal packet, encouraging her to take up swimming.

She glared back at it. 'Get a life!'

She continued munching her cornflakes as she scowled round the breakfast table on a grey February morning. Ellie, her elder sister, had been given a mobile for her thirteenth birthday and was busy texting her friends while her breakfast got cold. Dad was sipping coffee and reading something about rocks – surprise, surprise. And Mum was frying eggs and bacon, and listening to a man on the radio talking about diseases of ladybirds and predicting a disastrous year for gardeners.

'Welcome to Putney in the twenty-first century,' groaned Lucy.

'Where's Kal?' asked Mum.

The door burst open and slammed against the radiator. Caspar, Lucy's cat let out a yowl and dived under the table.

'Oh, for goodness sake,' muttered Ellie.

'Kal, do try and not charge around like that,' said Mum, more out of habit than expectation.

Kal waved a letter. 'Look! Someone's written to Mum from Tanzania.'

'Rubbish!' said Ellie.

'No, see the stamp.'

'Where's Tanzania?' asked Lucy.

'Near Australia,' said Kal.

'That's Tasmania,' scoffed Ellie. 'Tanzania's in East Africa, just south of the equator.'

Lucy perked up. The twenty-first century was looking brighter.

'Do we know anyone in Tanzania?' asked Dad.

'Reuben Kalima,' suggested Kal.

'What? The Olympic medallist?' cried Ellie.

'Well, I sort of know him.'

'Just because you can run and have been nicknamed after him, hardly means you…'

'Good Lord,' said Mum, and had to sit down.

'Mum, my breakfast!' yelled Kal.

'Oh no!' Mum leapt up, grabbed the smoking pan, thrust it into the sink, and turned on the cold tap. There was a great hiss, and the kitchen filled with steam.

'You're not supposed to do that,' said Lucy. 'We learned that in food technology.'

Mum flapped ineffectually at the steam; then turned on the extractor fan, and turned off the stove and the man who was droning on about ladybirds.

Kal peered into the sink. 'Yuk! I'm not eating that!'

'It's all right, Kal, I'll cook you some more,' said Mum. 'I'm afraid I was distracted by the letter.'

'Who's it from?' asked Lucy.

'Don't you have a cousin in Tanzania?' said Ellie.

Mum nodded. 'Let's see, Craig must be nearly thirty by now. What a lovely surprise; we haven't been in touch for ages but listen: "*Dear Sarah, Please excuse my writing to you out of the blue like this, but I wonder if I could ask a big favour of David…*'

'Me?' said Dad.

'Just listen. "*I now manage a wildlife ranch in Tanzania…*"

'Wow,' murmured Lucy, who wanted to be a wildlife vet.

"*…and am developing a programme of conservation that integrates the needs of the wildlife with those of the local Maasai people and their livestock…*"

'What does integrate mean?' asked Lucy.

'Don't interrupt,' said Ellie.

'It means that both the needs of wildlife and local people will be considered together,' said Mum. 'But this is the really exciting bit: "*However, we are finding it increasingly difficult to meet the rising costs of running the ranch, and need to explore ways to increase our income. If David could spare us some of his valuable time from work, we would very much like to employ him as a geology consultant to evaluate the area and identify potential resources that might be exploited. We believe, for example, there may be deposits of commercially valuable minerals in some parts of the ranch…*"

'What sort of minerals?' asked Dad.

'He doesn't say.'

'Probably diamonds,' said Lucy, 'they're found in Africa.'

Ellie snorted.

'What do you think?' asked Mum, folding the letter.

'Well, I'm blowed,' said Dad.

'Mum, it's brilliant!' cried Lucy. 'Will you go, Dad?'

Dad picked up the cereal packet and inspected the rat. 'I'll have to see.'

'We could all go,' suggested Kal.

'Why not?' said Mum. She turned to Dad. 'David, didn't you say there was a geology congress in Tanzania that you were thinking of attending?'

'Yes, but…'

'Please!' cried Lucy.

'Craig does say that we would all be welcome at Simba Ranch,' added Mum.

Six weeks later, Dad came back with the tickets.

Kal had never seen a crime committed – boys nicking crisps from other people's lunch boxes didn't count. Now, here he was on the terrace in front of a Tanzanian hotel surrounded by people who spoke a language he couldn't understand, and two of them – only a few paces away – were about to steal a valuable Range Rover: a silver V8 supercharged Vogue SE diesel.

An important-looking man in a suit, whom Kal thought looked like a toad, had driven up in the vehicle, parked in a no-waiting area, and gone into the hotel. Kal looked frantically around but there was no sign of him. He glanced back at the two men: one was tall and wearing a dirty t-shirt that proclaimed: "*Jesus saves*"; the other was more thickset and had some sort of red blanket over his shoulder.

Kal had to do something. Mum and Lucy were rabbiting on to Craig, who had his back to the scene, about how exciting it was coming to East Africa for the first time. Dad, who had gone off to register for his geology congress, was somewhere inside the hotel. Ellie, as always, was texting on her mobile.

'What's the matter with this stupid thing?' she muttered.

The thickset man gazed casually around and edged nearer to the vehicle. His companion lounged against a wall watching the entrance of the hotel.

Kal tried to catch Craig's attention.

'Kal,' snapped Lucy, 'I'm talking to Craig; don't interrupt!'

The thickset man was now in the vehicle. He was in the driving seat. He had started the engine.

'But there's two…'

'Two what?'

The important-looking man had come onto the terrace. Kal made frantic gestures and pointed at the Range Rover, but the man merely glared, turned on his heel and climbed into the passenger's seat.

Kal's voice trailed off. 'Nothing.'

'Honestly!'

The other man then climbed into the back, and the three of them drove off together. Kal was left gaping after them. Men in smart suits – even if they did look like toads – didn't allow themselves to be driven off in valuable Range Rovers by scruffy men. But was it a crime? Perhaps he'd imagined it – the jet lag, the overnight flight from London – but he knew he hadn't.

Lucy stroked the little dog sitting on her lap. 'It's just so nice to be here, Fupi – actually here, in Tanzania,' she whispered.

Fupi, Craig's terrier, who had immediately attached herself to Lucy, wagged her tail in agreement.

'I can't wait to get to Simba,' murmured Lucy.

Simba! Until now it had just been a name, a dot on a map in the middle of Africa. Now, Lucy, Ellie, and Kal would be there before the day was out, actually staying on the wildlife conservation ranch that Craig managed.

Mum told the children that they had met Craig when they were small, but Lucy couldn't remember. Now as she studied him chatting to Mum, he looked just as she expected: short fair hair, bleached even lighter by the sun; blue eyes that sparkled when he smiled (which he did often); and tanned face and arms – a sort of bronzy copper. She surreptitiously compared her own arms; they were white and smeary from sun cream. Yuk! She rubbed in the cream, but her arms stayed white. How long did it take to get that bronzy copper tan? They only had a few weeks.

People said that the Bartlett children all looked similar with their brown hair and brown eyes. Lucy thought that was rubbish: her hair was short; Ellie's was longer and either spiked up with gel or sleeked down with conditioner; while Kal's... Kal's was long and always untidy. So they didn't look similar. Also they...

'Who's that?' asked Mum, interrupting Lucy's daydream. She was indicating a tall man in dark glasses who seemed to be waving in their direction.

Craig turned in his seat. 'He's a policeman,' he said, his face lighting up. He waved to the man to come and join them.

'Perhaps he's come about the Range Rover,' blurted Kal.

'The Range Rover? What Range Rover?'

'I just thought he might sort of... that is I...' Kal was rescued by the arrival of the policeman at their table.

'Hey, man, good to see you,' said Craig. 'Grab a seat.' He pulled out a chair and signalled to a waiter to bring the newcomer a drink.

'So what brings you to Arusha?' the policeman asked.

'I've been collecting these good people from the airport,' said Craig.

Mum rose to her feet, looking flustered. 'I'm Sarah Bartlett, Craig's cousin.' She gave a twittery sort of breathless laugh. 'He's invited us all to stay on Simba ranch; isn't that lovely? This is Ellie who's thirteen and her sister Lucy who's eleven, and this is Alan but we call him Kal, after Reuben Kalima the famous runner from your country.' She came up for air.

'Is that so?' said the man, smiling.

Lucy squirmed in her seat – this was *so* embarrassing.

'Yes, Kal's only twelve but he's a very good runner; he's got the right build, you see. Rather like yours, I suppose.' Another gulp of air. 'I'm sorry, I didn't catch your name.'

The man held out his hand. 'My name is Reuben Kalima. Welcome to Tanzania.'

'Oh no!' Mum sat down suddenly. 'I thought Craig said you were a policeman.'

'I *am* a policeman.'

Kal gazed awestruck. 'Are you really Reuben Kalima, who won the Olympic steeplechase?'

Reuben removed his dark glasses and smiled.

'You are,' breathed Kal, his falling mouth open.

'Don't stare!' hissed Ellie. 'It's rude.'

Kal snapped his mouth shut but continued his mesmerized stare.

'I wish I could join you on Simba,' said Reuben, sitting down next to Mum. 'It's a great place.'

'Does *simba* mean lion king?' asked Lucy.

'No, you idiot – *simba* means lion,' said Ellie, who had finally given up with her mobile, realising she couldn't get a signal.

'We took the children to see a wonderful musical,' explained Mum.

Reuben smiled politely.

'Do you have lions on the ranch, Craig?' asked Lucy.

'Plenty,' said Craig, 'but that's not how it got its name; the house is built near a hill which the local people think looks like a resting lion. They call it, *Mlima ya Simba*.'

'The Hill of the Lion,' murmured Ellie.

'*Unajua kiswahili?*' cried Craig, 'you know Swahili?'

Ellie blushed and looked at her hands. 'I, er… borrowed some tapes from the library.'

'Hey, man, that's great!'

'Ellie's very good at languages,' said Mum.

'Mum!'

'But you are.'

'It's because she eats lots of fish,' explained Lucy, 'but it doesn't seem to work for me.'

Craig and Reuben laughed.

'Do the lions come near the house?' asked Kal.

'Depends what you mean,' said Craig, 'we haven't actually had them inside, but I once found one sleeping on the veranda. He got quite a fright when I tripped over him in the dark – so did I!'

'Oh dear.' Mum's hand flew to her mouth. 'I do hope it's safe.' She blinked, bit her lip, and took a quick sip of her drink.

Reuben turned to Craig. 'Has that trouble you were having been sorted out?'

Craig shook his head. 'I wish I could find out who was behind it.'

'Trouble,' said Mum in alarm. 'What are we talking about?'

'Oh, just some local nonsense,' said Craig, waving a dismissive hand. 'Nothing you need worry about.'

Mum looked uncertain.

'There's trouble back at the ranch,' drawled Kal, imitating a cowboy on a crumby film the family had watched over Christmas.

Everyone laughed, and Mum finally relaxed. She and the girls started chatting.

Reuben finished his drink. 'I'm afraid I have to leave,' he said, getting to his feet. 'You'll let me know, Craig, if you need any help.'

'Sure.'

Kal scrabbled in his bag; the only thing he could find was his boarding pass. 'Do you think I could have your autograph?' he asked breathlessly, handing it with a pen to Reuben.

'Of course.' Reuben smiled and wrote: "*From one Kal to another. Welcome to Tanzania, Reuben.*" He shook hands with everyone, and left.

Kal gazed at his boarding pass in disbelief. 'That is mega cool.'

'Ah, there you are,' said Dad, bustling up. 'I thought I'd lost you.'

'Where have you been?' asked Mum.

'I've been organising our room, Sarah: number eighty-seven on the other side of the courtyard at the back and I've had the luggage sent across.' He looked round at the family. 'Everyone okay?'

'Yes, Dad,' chorused the children.

'David, how you doin', buddy?' A man in baggy shorts that exposed his sunburned knees clapped Dad on the back.

'Vernon!' cried Dad, 'I was hoping you'd be coming to the congress; I've been meaning to ask you about your recent paper on…'

'We're going to stay on a wildlife ranch,' said Lucy.

'Well you enjoy it, little lady.'

'I'm going to be a wildlife vet when I…'

'This is my family,' said Dad, frowning at Lucy's interruption.

'Hi, folks, you all having a good time?' said the man.

The children nodded.

'Professor Vernon er… um is an American colleague of mine, a world expert on subduction of continental plates,' said Dad.

'What's seduction?' asked Lucy.

'Subduction *not* seduction!'

Kal sniggered.

Dad glared at him, then took his colleague's arm. 'Vernon, there are a couple of points I'd like to clarify with you about your hypothesis on tectonic…' He turned to the family. 'Excuse me, I have to…' He led his colleague away.

'Bye, Dad,' murmured Ellie, 'nice knowing you.'

'Bye, Professor Er Um,' said Kal.

'These geologists and their rocks!' muttered Mum. 'It's all they can think about once they get together.'

Craig smiled. 'We hope, though, that David can put his knowledge to good use after the congress.'

'Are there really diamonds on Simba Ranch?' asked Lucy. 'Ellie wants a diamond necklace.'

'Go well with that t-shirt,' murmured Kal.

'Just shut up!' cried Ellie.

Craig laughed. 'I'm afraid, Ellie, you may be disappointed. But we think there is something of interest…'

'What?' cried Lucy.

'That's what we need your Dad to tell us. But…' Craig paused. 'If he doesn't find anything, we might…'

'Might what?'

'We might struggle on as a cattle ranch. If not, we'd have to close down; we couldn't pay the staff, couldn't maintain the roads; poachers would come and kill the animals; the Maasai people with whom we share the ranch might have to move away – that sort of thing.'

'That sounds awful.'

'Yes, Lucy; it does.' He got to his feet. 'But let's not spoil your holiday. Come on, time to go.'

Mum began fussing. 'Do be careful, children. Will you be all right on your own while your father and I stay for the congress?'

'We'll be fine,' said Kal.

'I do hope so. Have you remembered your toothbrushes?'

'Mu-um!'

'Oh well… Now, do exactly as Craig tells you.' Mum hugged each of them in turn. 'And don't forget to put on plenty of sun cream; the sun can be…'

They were out of earshot.

'Craig, where are we going?' asked Ellie, as the dilapidated taxi threaded its way through Arusha's noisy traffic.

'To collect my plane.'

'Your plane!' cried Kal. 'You've got your own plane?'

'Sure – best way to get around out there. Do you fly?'

Kal hesitated. 'Well, I er, can sort of fly a Tornado.'

'What rubbish!' said Ellie. 'You can operate a Play Station from the sofa.'

'It's more than you can do,' retorted Kal. 'You crash every time.'

'I'd be the same,' said Craig, chuckling. 'I reckon flying a Cessna is a bit easier than a Tornado.'

Their driver turned off the main road, through a gateway, and stopped in front of a white building. Craig paid him while the children collected their bags and Lucy fitted a lead to Fupi's collar. Then they all followed Craig through the building to where some planes, mostly small single-engine, were parked in neat rows.

'This is it,' said Craig, stopping by one of the planes. Fupi wagged her tail expectantly.

'Cool,' said Kal.

'It looks ever so small,' said Ellie.

'You sound just like Mum,' said Kal.

'No, I don't!'

Craig slid one of the front seats forward to make room for them. 'Climb aboard – Ellie and Lucy first,' he said, taking Fupi from Lucy.

Ellie was right. The plane was small – very small. They struggled into the awkward space with its two seats, clipped on their belts and looked nervous.

Craig passed Fupi to Lucy; then slid the front seat back into position. 'Right, Kal, you sit there.' He indicated one of the two front seats, each facing a set of controls. He climbed in beside Kal, passed him some headphones and shut the door. 'We'll run through the controls and checks,' he said. 'Probably not as complicated as a Tornado,' he added with a grin.

Kal tried to grin in response, but it came out as a sickly smile.

'This switch operates the internal light,' said Craig, 'and this one the landing lights, fuel primer here, master electrical switch, spare set of ignition keys tucked under the visor here...'

Ellie and Lucy exchanged anxious glances. Surely he wasn't going to let Kal...

The noise was deafening as Craig started the engine. He turned in his seat. 'You guys, ready?' he shouted. 'Seat belts secure?'

The girls nodded.

And that was it. In no time, they were off the ground and flying out over the Arusha National Park. Craig banked the plane round as they climbed higher, and then pointed. 'Ngurdoto Crater,' he shouted, indicating the extinct volcano beneath them. Its slopes were covered in thick forest, and the crater, once a cauldron of molten rock, was now a green oasis. In the middle were, what appeared to Lucy, to be greyish mice.

'Elephants,' mouthed Craig, above the noise of the plane.

Lucy couldn't believe it. Then she saw some ants that were apparently buffaloes. Things they had previously seen just on television were there – right below them!

Craig pointed out to the right of the plane. 'Mount Kilimanjaro,' he shouted, 'highest mountain in Africa.'

'What's the white on the top?' Lucy shouted back.

'Snow.'

'But we're in the tropics.'

'It's around six thousand metres – cold enough for permanent snow.'

Craig set a course due west and headed towards a mountain in the far distance. 'That's the Ngorongoro Crater,' he shouted. 'Simba Ranch is some seventy miles beyond. About two hours to go.'

Lucy settled back in her seat and yawned. Fupi was already asleep on her lap, and before Lucy realised, her overnight flight caught up with her and she dozed off.

She woke and looked around. Her eyes widened. She gave a cry of alarm, which woke Ellie.

'What is it?'

Lucy pointed.

Ellie screamed.

CHAPTER 2

Serval

WILDLIFE VET

Craig looked up from the newspaper he was reading. 'What's the problem?'

The girls were making inarticulate noises and pointing at Kal.

'Kal's working the controls... he's... he's flying the plane!' shouted Lucy in a strangled voice.

Craig nodded and went back to his paper.

Kal turned and grinned.

'Keep your eyes on the road!' shouted Lucy. 'The sky, I mean.'

'He's not safe!' yelled Ellie.

The girls clung to the backs of the seats in front.

Craig turned and smiled at them. 'You're okay,' he mouthed. 'I'm keeping an eye on him.'

Gradually, Lucy relaxed, and when she realised that the tiny plane was not about to fall out of the sky, she turned her attention to the scenery below. Craig pointed out Lake Manyara in the far distance and just to the south the magnificent Ngorongoro crater – another extinct volcano. After that, there was very little sign of civilisation except the occasional hut and one or two dirt roads leading, as far as Lucy could tell, nowhere. Then, having reached the middle of nowhere, Craig said they'd arrived.

Lucy saw a small patch of green with a bungalow and some other buildings beyond. 'Is that it?'

Craig nodded, took over the controls from Kal and banked the plane round.

Lucy and Fupi pressed their noses against the window. Giraffes! Three of these beautiful creatures were nibbling at the tops of some trees, completely ignoring the plane coming in to land.

Craig lined up on a strip of sandy ground beyond the buildings. Some zebras that had been standing on the strip galloped off when he revved the engine.

The plane's wheels rattled on the bumpy ground; trees and bushes flashed by; the plane quickly slowed and they came to a stop. Craig switched off the engine and everyone climbed out.

'What a beautiful place,' said Ellie.

Fupi was scurrying around sniffing but kept coming back to the children, panting and wagging her tail as if to say: welcome to Simba.

'This is cool,' said Kal.

'Not a bad spot,' agreed Craig. 'See, there's the hill: *Mlima ya Simba.*'

'It doesn't look much like a lion to me,' said Lucy.

'Don't blame me,' said Craig, laughing, 'I didn't name it.'

A Land Rover was coming towards them, but none of them – not even Kal – had seen one like this: the cab and all the windows (other than the windscreen) had been removed; there were dents in the wings and doors, and the paint was falling off. But it wasn't so much the vehicle that attracted their attention, as the driver. He had a red-and-white check cloth over one shoulder, a bead necklace round his neck and a matching bracelet on his wrist. In his ear lobes (which were greatly stretched) were some elaborate bead earrings, and his hair had been braided in long tight plaits and smeared with, what Lucy later learned, was fat and red ochre. When he got down from the vehicle, she saw that his sandals were made from old car tyres, and round his waist was a leather belt, from which hung a wicked-looking sword. Craig told Kal that it was called a *simi*.

'This is Joel,' said Craig, 'he's our head game scout.'

The only Swahili that Lucy had learned was "hello", and she now greeted the smiling man. '*Jambo*, Joel.'

'*Jambo*, Lucy, *habari yako?*'

'Er.'

'That means "how are you?"' whispered Ellie. 'You say "*nzuri*". It means "fine".'

'Er, *nzuri*,' said Lucy.

'Very good, Lucy,' said Joel. 'You will soon speak Swahili.'

'I'm not sure about that.'

He smiled and shrugged.

Ever since they heard they were coming to Tanzania, Lucy had been learning about the wildlife from the books Mum had bought her. She was expecting things to be a bit like home, where she would get all excited if there was a deer half a mile away in a field, or if a fox crossed the road in front of the car headlights, or if she saw a woodpecker in Richmond Park. But here – she couldn't believe it. There were so many different kinds of animal; they were only a few paces from the vehicle and taking no notice of it. There were more giraffes, some baboons and warthogs, and she thought she recognised impala and a bushbuck (both rather like deer) – but she'd have to check these in her books.

'Craig, this is fantastic!' she cried, 'I can't believe it. I'm going to write down everything I see.'

He turned and smiled. 'Good for you, Lucy.'

'You'll have to help me, though, there's so much.'

'Sure.'

The vehicle came clear of the trees, and there was a stone and wooden bungalow with a brilliant orange creeper cascading over the roof. Chattering sunbirds were searching amongst its flowers with their curved beaks, the sun glinting on their plumage. In front of the veranda, that ran the length of the house, was a green lawn on which two orange and black birds were probing with long curved beaks. Lucy recognised them as hoopoes.

A tall lady came down the steps of the veranda to meet them. She had wrinkly brown skin and was wearing a flowery cotton dress. Craig's mother, Mrs Elliott, reminded Lucy of Mrs Sandford, their headmistress, but she smelled of wood smoke rather than school dinners.

'Come and have some refreshment, children, you must be tired after your long journey,' she said, leading the way up the steps to the veranda.

'*Come and have some refreshment, children,*' whispered Ellie, mimicking Mrs Elliott's headmistress voice, and starting Lucy in a fit of giggles.

'Barking,' muttered Kal. 'Hey, what's that?'

'It's a hyrax,' cried Lucy, 'I've got a picture in one of my books.'

A greyish brown animal, like a large guinea pig, scampered up the steps ahead of them and jumped onto a chair beside an elderly black Labrador that grinned and thumped its tail.

'He's Pimbi, one of my babies,' said Mrs Elliott.

The children looked at her uncertainly.

'An orphan whose mother was killed by an eagle,' she explained.

'Have you got any other orphan animals, Mrs Elliott?' asked Lucy.

'Lucy, you must call me Diana.'

Imagine, Mrs Sandford saying: "*You must call me Belinda*", thought Lucy.

'Yes, Lucy,' said Diana, 'we have quite a collection. You can help me feed them later if you like.'

'Yes please, Mrs Ellio… Diana, that is.'

A large lady wearing a headscarf, a green dress, and a broad smile, appeared carrying a tray with drinks and a plate of biscuits.

'Martha,' said Diana, 'these are the Bartlett children: Ellie, Lucy and Kal, who are staying with us for a few weeks.'

Martha put the tray down and her smile broadened as she came and greeted them each in turn.

'Martha is our housekeeper,' explained Diana. 'Her husband, Samson, is assistant manager in charge of the cattle on the ranch.'

'Right, grab your drinks and some seats,' said Craig, after more hand shaking had been completed.

'Is that a lion?' asked Kal.

'Where?' Lucy leapt up.

'There.' Kal was pointing at a skin lying over the back of Lucy's chair.

'Don't do that, Kal!' Lucy gave him a dirty look.

'Yes,' said Craig, 'Mother shot it.'

The three children stared at her open-mouthed.

'Well, he was killing the cattle,' said Diana.

'You shot a lion!' exclaimed Kal.

Diana nodded.

'Imagine Granny shooting a lion,' said Lucy.

'What – in Richmond Park?' said Kal.

'No, don't be a twit! You know what I mean.'

'It was years ago,' explained Diana, 'soon after I married your mother's uncle Peter, and we started farming in Tanzania. Lions were quite a problem and that one got so bold we were worried it might start attacking people.'

'Do you shoot lions, Craig?' asked Kal.

'No ways – we're a conservation ranch. We keep a couple of rifles to take with us in the bush, but we've only had to use them to scare animals off – never to...' His voice trailed off as a powerfully built man wearing jeans and a t-shirt hurried onto the veranda and whispered in his ear. Craig frowned as he listened.

The children looked uneasily at each other.

The man finished talking to Craig and turned to the children. His face broke into a warm smile. 'My name is Samson. Welcome to Simba.'

There was more hand shaking. By now, Lucy's hand was beginning to ache.

'Some men have brought in an injured animal,' said Samson. 'They are hoping Craig can treat it.'

'What sort of animal?' asked Lucy, her eyes widening.

Craig stood up. 'Let's find out.' He led them through the house to the back door. Two men were sitting on their haunches under a tree. They were wearing the same traditional Maasai clothing as Joel, and their spears were stuck in the ground beside them. A sack lay nearby, but whatever was inside was keeping very still.

Craig called to them in Swahili.

'*Chui*,' replied one of the men.

Ellie gasped.

'Ellie, what is it?' cried Lucy.

'It's a leopard; they've brought a leopard. Is that right, Craig?'

Craig nodded. 'They say some children saw a young leopard near their goats, and one of them threw a spear at it. When they wounded it, they got frightened and told their father – he's the taller one.'

'Why were they frightened?' asked Lucy.

'Because they know I'm trying to protect the animals and they thought I'd be angry if I found out.'

Lucy looked back at the sack. 'It's not moving.'

'Come,' said Craig. He picked up the sack and led them through a clump of trees to a collection of pens within which was an assortment of young animals. 'Mother's zoo,' he said, waving his hand airily round the pens. 'All orphans that have been rescued. Most of them arrived in sacks.'

'What's going to happen to them?' asked Lucy.

'As soon as they're old enough, they'll be released back to the wild in a safe part of the ranch.'

Joel, who was in one of the pens bottle-feeding a young zebra, waved to them. He grinned, finished the feeding, and came and joined them.

'In here,' said Craig, indicating an empty pen. 'You kids better wait outside.'

Joel joined Craig in the pen, took his *simi* and carefully cut open the sack. A beautiful spotted animal was lying there not moving.

'A serval!' exclaimed Craig. 'It's not a leopard.'

'It's dead,' said Lucy, 'that is so sad.' She could see a horrible red gash down the animal's chest exposing muscle and bone beneath.

Craig peered into the animal's mouth; then felt its chest.

'No, it's still alive – just.' He stood up. 'Lucy, you told me you wanted to be a wildlife vet. Now's your chance.'

'What!'

'I'll help. Come in. This guy won't run off.'

Lucy entered the pen and knelt beside the serval. She put a hand on its chest and felt a fluttering heartbeat and the occasional gasping breath. 'Please get better,' she whispered.

'If he stops breathing,' said Craig, 'push down on the chest a few times.'

'Like we learned in Guides in first aid?'

'Exactly like that. I'll be as quick as I can.' He called to Ellie and they ran back to the house.

Lucy inspected the horrible wound. Flies were buzzing round. She waved them away. The serval's breathing was very shallow, and every time it exhaled, a little spout of pink froth came from the wound in its chest. She nestled her head against the animal's soft fur and could hear its failing heart. 'Don't die,' she whispered.

Craig was back. Behind him was Ellie, carrying a bowl of hot water with antiseptic in it.

'Right, let's see what we can do.' Craig opened the box he had been carrying and Lucy saw that it was full of instruments, syringes, bandages, and bottles of different medicines.

'Long way from hospital here – we have to be able to deal with emergencies,' said Craig, taking out a bottle and drawing some liquid from it into a syringe. 'This is local anaesthetic. I know the guy looks peaceful, but we don't want to risk it.' He passed the syringe to Lucy. 'There you go.'

Lucy was aghast. 'But, I've never...'

'I'll hold the wound open,' said Craig, 'just squirt a small amount over it. Good. Now, put the needle here into the muscles and the skin. Great. Keep going – all round the wound.'

Lucy was concentrating so hard, she didn't have time to

think how horrible the wound looked, or is he going to die, or how uncomfortable it was kneeling in the dirt?

'That'll do,' said Craig. 'Now while we wait for the local to work, you can clean the wound.'

Ellie placed the bowl of water beside Lucy.

Lucy picked off some bits of grass then washed away the dirt as well as she could. Craig passed her a sterile swab. 'Put that over the hole, stop the air getting into his chest – that's his main problem.'

Lucy held the swab in place with one hand and continued cleaning the rest of the wound using her free hand.

'Okay, take the swab away,' said Craig, who was now holding a curved needle in a pair of forceps.

Lucy removed the swab and Craig skilfully sewed the two sides of the hole together.

'I think his breathing's getting stronger,' said Lucy.

Craig opened the serval's mouth. 'Good, and see the tongue's looking a better colour – it was bluish before.' He turned back to his box and passed a container to Lucy. 'Antibiotic powder: sprinkle it over the wound before we sew up the skin. It's impossible to work under sterile conditions here. Let's hope it works.' He began closing the wound with stitches, while Lucy assisted by holding up the edges of the skin with another pair of forceps. Craig passed Lucy the needle. 'You do the last stitch,' he said.

Lucy gulped. Her stitch didn't look as neat as Craig's but she was really pleased she hadn't made a mess of it.

'Lucy, the wildlife vet,' said Craig.

'Thanks, Craig.' She stood up blinking and hoped Craig wouldn't notice the tears. She felt really proud.

Craig injected some antibiotic into the serval's neck. Lucy then helped him carry it on the sack to another pen that was fully enclosed.

'They climb nearly as well as leopards,' he said, 'we don't want him getting out before we're ready.'

'Will he be all right?' she asked.

'If he gets through the night.'

'We need to give him a name.' Lucy furrowed her brow. 'What's Swahili for serval?'

'Mondo.'

'That's it!'

Craig smiled. 'Good name.'

'Can I stay with him for a bit?'

'Sure. Joel will be around; give a shout if you need any help. I'll get you some water. Trickle small amounts into his mouth; just make sure he swallows.'

Lucy nodded. She sat down on the ground beside Mondo, and gently lifted his head into her lap.

When Craig and the others came back an hour later, Lucy and Mondo were in the same position. His eyes were still closed, but he was purring softly.

CHAPTER 3

Ground Hornbill

LUCY GOES BIRDWATCHING

The children were staying in a log cabin some way from the main house. Ellie told them it was called a *banda*. There were three adjacent rooms – one each – and a shared veranda.

That night, Lucy lay in the dark thinking about the wonderful day they had had, and the amazing people they had met – and of course, Mondo. And to think, this time yesterday they were travelling to the airport on a cold wet night in what was supposed to be summer. Now, here they were in the middle of Africa and it was a hundred degrees warmer. She listened to the strange sounds of the night: some were birds, some were mammals, some were insects, some were even frogs, and some were the wind caressing the trees and grass. She didn't know many of the sounds at the time, but over the next few weeks, she learned to recognise the calls of nightjars, stone curlews, zebras, lions,

cicadas and owls, but on that first night, they were just sounds –
a kind of bush orchestra that lulled her to sleep.

The next morning, the bush orchestra sounded very different
– as though all the birds in Africa were trying to out-sing each
other and wake her up. How Kal could sleep through that racket,
she had no idea. She could hear his snores coming from the next
room.

There was a knock on the door, and Martha entered
carrying a cup of tea.

'*Jambo*, Lucy, how did you sleep?'

'*Jambo*, Martha, very well.'

'Lucy, you should say *nzuri sana*; it means, very well or very
good,' said Martha, setting the cup beside Lucy's bed.

'*Nzuri sana*. How's that?'

'*Nzuri sana*!' cried Martha, clapping her hands. 'Craigi
wants to make an early start this morning, and has asked me to
wake you all up.'

'I was awake –it's brill here.'

'Brill?' She looked puzzled.

'Martha, it's not very good English; it's slang.'

But Martha wasn't listening. As she went out of the room to
call the other two, Lucy could hear her murmuring "brill, brill"
to herself.

Lucy had a quick shower, got dressed and ran across to the
main house. Martha was setting the breakfast table, and Craig
was in his office at the end of the veranda talking to someone on
a radio – they didn't have a telephone at Simba and mobile signals
were unreliable. He saw her and waved. She waved back and went
to help Martha lay the table.

'And how's Lucy today?' asked Craig, coming out of his
office.

'*Nzuri sana*.'

'Hey, man!'

'Martha's been teaching me some Swahili.'

'Great!'

'How's Mondo?'

'Let's go and see.' Craig led her to the animal pens.

Lucy was terrified at what she might find: that beautiful animal stretched out stiff and cold on the ground. Her heart was pounding as they approached Mondo's enclosure. He was lying on some straw in one corner.

'Mondo,' she called. 'Mondo.'

The serval put up its head.

'Craig, he's alive! He's going to be all right.'

'Looks like it. Joel tells me he's already eaten some food. See, and there's no swelling round the wound. You did a good job, Lucy.'

She looked into his face and grinned. 'He looks quite like a leopard.'

Craig nodded. 'We don't often see them on the ranch. That's why the guys were confused.'

'Would he have killed the goats?'

'Unlikely; they normally go for rodents, but the children don't understand that.'

'Do the Maasai often attack the wild animals?'

Craig shook his head. 'No ways! Provided their own animals are not threatened, they usually leave them alone. I guess this guy just came a bit too close.' He smiled. 'Come on, let's go and get some breakfast.'

They returned to the veranda, where Martha had produced a mountain of food, which Kal was fast demolishing.

'Craig, what's happening today?' asked Kal, through a mouthful of bacon and eggs.

'We're going on safari, over there, to the Seki Hills.' Craig pointed into the distance. 'I want to check them out before your dad arrives, but it means spending the night there.'

'What – camping?' cried Lucy.

Craig nodded. 'Joel's loading the gear just now.'

'Great!'

'But we're going there to work.'

'What sort of work?' asked Kal, a note of wariness in his voice.

'A bit of flying and…'

'What!'

'I need to photograph the places we want your dad to survey, so while I'm taking the pictures you can help with the flying.'

'Awesome!'

Ellie arrived. Her hair had been spiked up with gel, and she was wearing combat jeans, a black t-shirt with a skull on it, and pink jewelled flip-flops.

'Great safari gear,' said Kal.

She pretended not to hear.

'We're going camping,' cried Lucy, 'and Kal's going to fly the plane… and… it's the sort of work that Craig does all the time.' She wasn't sure that was strictly true, but Craig didn't say anything. 'Isn't that great?'

Ellie shrugged. 'Whatever.'

'Don't you want to come?' cried Lucy.

'Not sure.'

'You're being a wimp,' said Kal.

'No, I'm not!'

Craig smiled at Ellie. 'You'll be fine. But you might, um… want to change your footwear.'

Ellie glared at him, said nothing; then left the table and went back to her *banda*.

'Is she okay?' asked Craig.

'Don't take any notice,' said Kal, 'she's just trying to be cool.'

'Right, guys, this is the plan,' said Craig, turning back to

Kal and Lucy, 'the main reason for going to the hills is to build an airstrip, so that…'

'An airstrip!' cried Lucy. 'How are you going to do that?'

'We find a flat space, clear a few rocks and trees, and…'

'And that's it?'

'More or less. We paint some stones to mark it out, and use it as our starting point when your dad gets here.' He helped himself to more coffee. 'While Kal and I are taking the photographs, Joel will take the Landy to another airstrip between here and the hills, where we'll meet him. Lucy and Ellie – if she decides to come…'

'She'll come, now she's made her point,' said Kal.

Craig smiled. 'You girls can come in the plane or go with Joel.'

'If Kal's going to be flying, we'll go with Joel,' said Lucy.

'Fine,' said Craig. 'Go and grab some clothes and your toothbrushes – remember what your mum said…'

'Oh that!' said Kal.

Craig raised his eyebrows. 'And Lucy, bring your binoculars and bird book; then we'll be off. I can hear Joel coming now.'

Lucy and Kal ran back to the *bandas*, and returned with Ellie – now wearing trainers, but still looking uncertain.

Lucy was relieved to see the Land Rover was different to the open one Joel had been driving yesterday. This one had a cab and a roof that was piled with bags and camping gear. Kal told her that the vehicle was a Defender one-ten, long-wheel-base – whatever that meant. Lucy knew that sort of thing interested him.

'The one we were in yesterday was a short-wheel-base,' said Kal.

'Oh,' said Lucy, not having a clue what he was talking about.

Craig's terrier was wagging her tail and looking expectantly between them.

'Is Shorty coming?' asked Kal.

'Her name's not Shorty!' cried Lucy. 'It's Fupi.'

'Same thing. Fupi means "short" in Swahili – Craig told me.'

'I don't care. Fupi's a much nicer name!' She scooped Fupi into her arms.

'Suit yourself,' said Kal. 'Anyway, what sort of dog is she? I bet you don't know that.'

'I do. She's called a Parson Russell Terrier. So there!'

'A what! I suppose that means she goes to church on Sundays.'

'Of course she doesn't. It's just that... Oh, for goodness sake, Kal!' Lucy turned to Craig. 'Can she come with us?'

Craig grinned. 'Of course. Fupi is my nose and ears in the bush; just as Joel is my eyes.'

∽⧟∾

Two hours later, Lucy, Ellie and Joel were sitting on their haunches under the shade of a tree, at the end of what Joel assured the girls, was an airstrip. Except for the absence of bushes or trees, the place didn't look to Lucy any different from the rest of the area. Some antelope were standing in the middle of it. Joel said they were Grant's gazelles. Lucy sat down with her back to the tree, got her binoculars out of their case, and studied them; they looked very like the impala she'd seen yesterday, but she supposed Joel knew what he was talking about. There wasn't much else to see around: a few bushes, some small brown birds pecking in the dust, and Craig's plane in the distance circling round the hills. It seemed to be taking ages.

Lucy gave a great sigh.

Ellie asked Joel to teach her some Maasai words, and the two of them went into a huddle as Joel began pointing out things to Ellie and telling her their Maasai names.

Lucy wondered what Mrs Sandford would think if we told

her that the "educational purpose" for which Mum had got us off school, involved crouching in the dirt in the middle of nowhere with a Maasai warrior wearing a *shuka* (which, to Lucy looked like a table-cloth) over his shoulder, and a wicked-looking sword (she remembered it was a *simi*), and learning a language that wouldn't be much help in school exams. So what? She shrugged and gazed around. The gazelles hadn't moved, but beyond them, a large black bird had appeared, striding across the ground. Before Lucy could find it through her binoculars, it walked behind some bushes and disappeared. She got up and walked towards the bushes. The gazelles trotted off. She turned and looked back at Ellie and Joel, who were still engrossed. Fupi was asleep under the Land Rover.

'I won't be a moment,' she said to herself.

The black bird had reappeared but was still striding off. She got a better view this time. It looked like a turkey. She stopped and checked her bird book. There was nothing about turkeys in the index. The bird continued its purposeful walk. Lucy hurried to get nearer. The bird was now in the open and had been joined by another. Lucy got a better view this time: the birds were about the size of turkeys, but they had large curved beaks and bright red faces. She crept up behind a thicket and checked in her book again. 'They're not storks,' she murmured, 'and they're not cranes.' The birds moved off. Lucy followed. It was exciting stalking them through the bush.

She settled down beside a termite mound and looked through her binoculars. The birds seemed to have caught something and were tossing it into the air. It was a lizard or possibly a snake. Poor thing!

Something startled the birds and they flew off. Lucy saw a large patch of white on their wings. She went back to her bird book. 'At last!' she cried, 'here we are: ground hornbills.'

She couldn't wait to tell Craig.

Kal couldn't imagine anything more exciting. Under Craig's watchful eye, he was flying a plane across the African bush. Tornado flying seemed very tame in comparison. The Cessna had dual controls, and while Craig operated the main set, Kal operated the others, the plane responding to his every movement; turning, banking, climbing. Whatever he did, the plane obeyed him. He could feel the g-force when he banked; he could feel his stomach sink when he climbed; he could hear and smell the engine; and he could feel the heat of the sun beating into the cockpit. At home, whatever he did to the controls, made no difference to the behaviour of the sofa. But here...

'Nearly there,' said a voice beside him.

Kal came out of his dream – but it wasn't a dream.

He looked across at Craig, and grinned.

'How's it going?' asked Craig.

'Wicked.'

Craig grinned back. 'See that hill,' he said, pointing ahead. 'Fly towards it, then turn; we'll fly a number of transects.'

'Roger that.'

For the next half hour, Kal flew back and forth over the hills, while Craig took a series of photographs. Kal was aware of Craig watching him and giving the occasional instruction, but there was no instance when he had to intervene.

Craig put his camera away. 'Time to find the others,' he said, 'over there.'

A few minutes later, Craig pointed down below, and Kal could see the Land Rover at the end of the airstrip. Two figures stood up and waved.

'Do you reckon you can land there?' asked Craig.

'You want me to land the plane!'

'Why not?'

'Cool.' Kal licked his lips, banked the plane round, lined up on the patch of ground in front, and moved the controls forward. The plane dipped, and as the ground came racing towards them Kal eased off the throttle and brought up the nose. He glanced quickly across at Craig, who nodded. The plane came lower. Kal held it steady as their speed dropped. He eased further off the throttle; it seemed almost as though the plane was now floating above the ground. There was a bump, then another, and they were down. Kal could hear the wheels of the undercarriage rattling over the rough ground. He shut down the throttle and applied the brakes. The plane coasted to a halt rather closer to the Land Rover than he intended. He switched off the engine, and looked across at Craig. 'That was awesome.'

'That was excellent,' said Craig. He opened his door and the two of them scrambled out.

'Where's Lucy?' called Craig, as Ellie and Joel came to greet them.

'She's just...' Ellie looked around. 'She was... Oh no!'

CHAPTER 4

Ant-lion

ANT-LIONS

Lucy packed her binoculars away, picked up her bird book and got to her feet. She shaded her eyes and looked in the direction of the hills where Craig and Kal had been flying, but couldn't see the plane. *Were* those the hills, though? She gazed around. Or, perhaps it was the hills to her left. They looked very similar. She thought she could hear a plane, but couldn't tell where the sound was coming from.

'This is silly,' she said to herself. 'Anyway, it doesn't matter, I must get back to Ellie and Joel.' She set off towards the termite mound from where she'd watched the hornbills. When she got to it, it didn't look quite right; this one had a hole in it where something had been digging. It was a large hole and flies were buzzing in and out.

She backed off – whatever had made the hole was still inside!

She tried to re-orientate. *There* was the termite mound; that was the one. When she reached it; it wasn't. She began to feel uneasy.

'There's nothing to worry about,' she said out loud. Hearing her own voice gave her reassurance. 'I shall navigate by the sun, like they tell you in books.'

The sun was directly overhead.

'Hmm. What about tracks, then? I'll follow my tracks and retrace my steps.' She peered at the sandy ground. She couldn't even see her tracks. The sand was so soft and dry that her footprints were just blurs amongst countless other blurs.

She sat down. 'Come on, Lucy, the important thing is to think – the others can't be that far away.' She didn't care that she was talking aloud to herself. She picked up a twig and began to draw in the sand. 'If the airstrip is here, and the hills where Craig and Kal were flying are here; that means I came this way.' She drew a line in the sand. 'So I must be about…'

Something threw sand at the twig.

She started back; then peered down – nothing. Something must have fallen from above. She looked up – there wasn't anything above, except blue sky and cotton wool clouds. She must have imagined it. She went back to her drawing. 'That means I'm…'

There it was again; this time there was no doubt. Something *was* throwing sand at her twig – something hidden in the ground. Then she noticed little pits in the sand all around. It was when her twig went near one of these that a spurt of sand was thrown at it. She had no idea what it was. 'Anyway,' she said, getting up, 'I'm not wasting any more time here. Craig will know.'

She glanced again at her drawing, looked around, saw the direction she should be heading and strode off. 'Five minutes – ten, at the most.'

She kept checking her watch. Twenty minutes later, there was no sign of the plane, or Craig, or Ellie, or Kal, or Joel, or Fupi. But she knew she was heading in the right direction. She began to run.

Something snorted, and crashed off through the bushes ahead – something big.

She stopped. She couldn't see what it was but she could still hear pounding hooves above the pounding of her heart. She slumped against a termite mound. She'd given up wondering whether it might be the one she was originally looking for. She closed her eyes and waited for her breathing and pounding heart to settle. Then tears began to form. She began to realise how hot it was; how similar everything looked; how she had no water; and how she was… how she was completely and utterly lost.

She cupped her hands round her mouth. 'Craig!'

A bird flew out of a nearby tree, but there was no answering cry.

'Craig! Craig, where are you?' Her cries were swallowed up in the bush. There wasn't even a reassuring echo from the surrounding hills. It was like pouring water into sand.

'Craig!'

Another bird – or perhaps the same one – started calling, as though mocking her.

She collapsed to the ground and let the tears flow. 'Ellie, Kal, where are you?' she sobbed.

She was lost. She would die of thirst. Vultures would eat her body. She had sometimes wondered what dying would be like. She'd never imagined it would be like this.

She heard pounding feet – that animal was coming back. She had nowhere to hide. This was it. She covered her head with her arms and tried to make herself as small as possible. The animal was upon her. It was snuffling round her head, trying to get at her face.

'Get away!'

The animal barked.

She froze. Gradually her mind began to register.

'Fupi?' She sat up. 'Fupi!' The little dog leapt into her arms and covered her face with a frantic slobbery tongue. 'Oh Fupi.'

'Are you all right, Lucy?' said a voice.

She looked up, and there was Joel, smiling. He was breathing hard.

She nodded, and blinked. She didn't care he could see she was crying.

~~~

'I guess I don't need to say anything,' said Craig, looking down at Lucy, who was slumped with her back against the Land Rover, sipping tea. The others were standing round her.

'No,' she said in a small voice. 'Craig, I'm really sorry.'

'We were so worried,' said Ellie.

'You could have been eaten by a lion,' said Kal.

Lucy nodded as she sat hunched up, her mug of tea cradled in her hands.

'Five more minutes,' said Craig, 'and I would have taken the plane up to search for you.'

Lucy gave a weak smile. 'I'm glad you care about me,' she said, and burst into tears.

'Oh, Lucy,' cried Ellie, kneeling down beside her sister and hugging her. 'Of course we care about you. We were just so worried.'

Craig gave Lucy his hankie. 'You okay?'

She sniffed and nodded; then blew her nose. 'How did Joel and Fupi find me?'

'The best trackers in Tanzania,' said Craig.

'You made a very good path,' said Joel, 'but you were going in circles.' He waved his hands around in the air.

'Lucy, it's so easily done,' said Craig, 'you keep thinking you recognise a twisted tree or strange-shaped termite mound. The trouble is, all the trees are twisted and all the termite mounds have strange shapes.'

'I know.'

'If it should ever happen again – and heaven forbid – orientate by the wind; that's one thing that tends to be constant here, always blowing from the same direction.'

She nodded; then perked up. 'But I did see some ground hornbills.'

Craig shook his head. 'Lucy, you're a case.'

She grinned. 'And something funny in the sand.'

'What?' asked Kal.

'Like sort of... Look there: those pits.' She pointed.

'Ant-lions,' said Craig, 'or rather the larvae of ant-lions. Fupi'll show you.' He pointed to one of the pits. 'Go on, Fupi!'

She sniffed where Craig was pointing and began to dig. She scooped out a wriggling creature with large jaws, which immediately tried to rebury itself.

Fupi went to pounce on it, but Craig held her back.

'These things live in pits like this for a number of years,' he explained, 'and any creature, such as an ant, that comes near, gets a face full of sand which knocks it into the pit; it slips down the side and into the jaws at the bottom.'

'Wicked,' said Kal.

Joel located an ant and steered it towards a pit with his *simi*. A puff of sand was thrown up; the ant slipped into the pit; there was a brief flash of jaws and the luckless ant disappeared.

'Do you get any bigger ones?' asked Ellie.

Craig shook his head.

'What do they turn into?' asked Lucy.

'Rather beautiful creatures like dragonflies that fly at night.'

'Are they dangerous?'

'Not at all. They're one of what we call the "little five".'

'I've heard of the big five,' said Lucy, now fully recovered from her ordeal.

'Okay, Lucy, what are the big five, then?' said Craig.

'Um – lion, leopard, rhino, elephant… and hippo.'

'Almost right: elephant and buffalo,' said Craig. 'The big five – what every tourist hopes to see.'

'I think the hippo should be on the list,' said Lucy, 'then it would be the big six.'

'I agree,' said Craig, 'but I'm afraid it's the big five – and the little five.'

'It's a wind-up,' said Kal.

'No ways – they're all real animals. You've got the ant-lion; then there's the leopard-tortoise, rhinoceros-beetle, elephant-shrew, and buffalo-weaver.'

'Yeah, and the hippopotamus-moth,' added Kal.

Craig chuckled. 'All right, don't believe me but…'

There was a sudden bark from Fupi. They looked up. A whirling roaring cloud of sand was rushing straight at them.

'Quick!' yelled Craig. 'You kids, all on the tail of the plane, shut your eyes, and hang on like crazy.'

They ran to the plane. Craig and Joel each grabbed a wing and the children clung to the tail. Fupi dived under the Land Rover. They watched in horror as this great monster roared towards them, throwing leaves, sticks, sand, and the occasional bird, into the air. It must have been over a hundred metres high. Then it hit them, pounding them with stinging particles of sand and tugging their clothes and hair. The plane bucked and kicked like a horse trying to break free. They kept their eyes screwed tight and tried to hold their breath while clinging on with all their strength.

CHAPTER 5

Eland

ELEPHANTS DON'T CHARGE

It was over as suddenly as it started. Cautiously, they opened their eyes and blinked, trying to get the gritty sand out. Fupi was shaking herself.

'What was *that*?' gasped Ellie, her gelled hair now full of sand.

'Dust devil,' said Craig. 'Well done, you lot – that could have been bad news if we hadn't held the plane down.'

'I won't be able to get clean for a week,' complained Ellie.

'Who cares?' said Kal.

'Typical!'

They watched the dust devil weaving its crazy way across the plain before it petered out some way off in the distance.

Craig called Joel to help him, and between them they fixed

anchor ropes to the wings and tail of the plane in case another one should come through.

'Right, guys – a snack,' said Craig, 'then we should get going.'

They sat in the shade of a tree and munched slices of watermelon, the juice running down their chins. Craig said the tree was called *Cordia* because you could use fibres from it to make cords or ropes. Joel, though, said his people called it Seki, and that's how the hills got their name. Then Craig said, in South Africa they called it the snot-berry – that of course appealed to Kal. Lucy found it very confusing.

Joel murmured something and pointed with his chin. An enormous antelope, like a large sandy cow with twisted horns, was watching them. Fupi pricked up her ears and kept very still.

'What is it, Craig?' breathed Lucy.

'Eland,' he whispered. 'Isn't he magnificent?'

The animal snorted, tossed its head and was gone. Lucy couldn't believe such a large animal could just vanish. She wondered if that was what she had frightened – or rather – what had frightened her?

'Was he real?' she asked.

Craig smiled. 'Largest antelope in Africa.'

'I wouldn't want to mess with him,' said Kal.

They finished their snack and Craig packed the things back into the Land Rover. Ellie went to climb inside.

'It's more fun on the roof,' said Craig, 'lots to see.'

'Is it safe?'

Kal gave her a withering look, scrambled onto the bonnet and then the roof, where he settled down amongst the camping things.

'It's cool. You get a great view,' he called.

Ellie and Lucy followed. Craig passed Fupi up to Lucy; then climbed up beside them.

'Okay, Joel,' he called. '*Tuende* – let's go.'

Driving cross-country was very slow because Joel had to

40

keep changing direction to go round rocks or trees, or avoid gullies, but gradually the hills crept nearer, and they could see patches of forest on the top.

Craig tapped on the roof of the vehicle and Joel stopped.

'Is this it?' asked Lucy.

'Not yet.' Craig pointed out to the left. 'Look there – just beyond those trees.'

'I can't see any… Wow, elephants!'

'They look awfully big,' said Ellie. 'Will they charge?'

'No,' said Craig, 'they're used to vehicles. See, they're taking no notice. If we were on foot we'd have to be more careful.'

He leaned over the edge of the roof. 'Drive a bit closer, Joel.'

'Please don't go too close,' said Ellie.

'It's okay, Joel's taking us down wind,' said Craig.

Joel stopped about fifty paces away and switched off the engine. The elephants were completely wild, yet here they were, having a snack, and apart from raising their trunks to try and sniff the visitors, taking almost no notice of the vehicle or the people on top.

'They've got indigestion,' said Kal.

'That rumbling noise, you mean?' said Craig.

'Sounds like Dad after he's had curry.'

'Kal, don't be so rude,' said Ellie.

'It's their way of communicating,' said Craig, 'saying they're content – like purring in a cat.'

'Some cat!'

'Why are they reddish?' asked Lucy, 'I thought elephants were grey.'

'That's the dust,' said Craig, 'murram – the stuff we use here to make the roads. The elephants blow it over themselves.'

'Ellie does that,' said Kal, 'says it dries the pores.'

'I most certainly do not,' snapped Ellie. 'Anyway, it's talcum powder, thank you very much.'

'Same thing.'

'Like you'd know!' She glared at Kal.

Lucy studied the elephants through her binoculars.

'It's a family group we know well,' said Craig. 'They spend most of their time on the ranch. See that one in the front with the tatty ears; she's probably about fifty; she's the matriarch…'

'*You must call me Diana*,' mimicked Ellie.

Lucy and Kal burst out laughing. Craig couldn't help joining in, and they could hear Joel hooting from inside the vehicle.

Ellie turned bright red. 'Oh no!' She put her hand to her mouth. 'Sorry, Craig.'

He grinned. 'I won't tell anyone.'

The elephants flapped their ears but otherwise continued to ignore them.

'As I was saying before I was so rudely interrupted,' continued Craig, 'she's the matriarch – her name is actually Belinda…'

'Oh no!' cried Lucy. 'That's our headmistress!' That started the girls off again.

'When you two have quite finished…' said Craig.

'They've got the same sort of ears,' spluttered Ellie. And off they went again.

'Nutters,' muttered Kal.

'The old elephant in the front is in charge of the herd,' said Craig, choosing his words carefully.

Lucy could hear occasional sniggers from Ellie and didn't dare look at her.

'It's a group of females and youngsters,' continued Craig. 'The males leave the herd when they become adult and go off and do their own thing.'

'Don't blame them,' said Kal. 'If I was…'

Joel started the engine and muttered something.

'What did he say?' asked Lucy.

'Moshi!' cried Craig.

'What's that?'

'Trouble, big time. Hold tight!'

Fupi dived down amongst the tents.

'Go, Joel, go!'

Joel slammed the Land Rover into gear, spun the steering wheel and tore off, the vehicle bumping and lurching over the rough ground. Those on the roof clung to the roof rack, the camping gear, anything they could grab hold of.

'What is it?' screamed Lucy.

'Behind you!' yelled Craig.

Lucy turned, and there was the most enormous elephant she could have imagined. Its ears were flat against its head, its trunk tucked back. It was no more than twenty paces behind – and it was catching them! She whimpered; then gasped as the branches off a low tree raked across the roof.

'Faster!' she yelled.

The Land Rover hit a bump.

Craig grabbed Kal as he was about to roll off. 'Hang on!'

They were now on smoother ground, and Joel was getting away. But the elephant wasn't slowing down. How could such a large animal run so fast? All its attention was focused on the vehicle. It was determined to destroy it and everyone in it. They came into an area of low bushes, and Joel had to keep swerving round them. The elephant, though, crashed straight through – like some enormous tank. Once more, it was gaining on them.

'No-o-o,' wailed Lucy.

Then, without warning, the elephant stopped, raised its trunk and gave an ear-splitting blast.

Joel didn't slacken his pace until they were a good two hundred metres clear; then brought the Land Rover to a halt but kept the engine running. The children were shaking, and Ellie was whimpering.

'Sorry about that,' said Craig. 'I didn't notice Moshi at the back of the herd.'

'I thought you said they wouldn't charge,' said Lucy, her face still white. She looked back at the elephant. It was weaving its body from side to side and flapping its ears. Its trunk was questing in the direction of the vehicle as it tried to pick up a scent.

'We haven't seen her for ages,' said Craig. 'Joel spotted her just in time.'

'What if he hadn't?' said Kal.

'Let's not think about it.'

The elephant thrashed the bushes with its trunk, gave a final blast of trumpeting; then turned, and disappeared into some trees.

'I knew I should have stayed behind,' cried Ellie.

'I just don't understand it,' said Craig. 'She used to be so peaceful; now she's really bad news – that's why Joel christened her Moshi.'

'What does it mean?' asked Kal.

'Smoke. You never know how it will behave.'

'That figures.'

'What happened to make her like that?' asked Lucy.

'I wish I knew,' said Craig, looking pensive. 'We'll have to warn the Maasai though, otherwise someone might get hurt – or worse.'

'Isn't there something you can do to make her better?' asked Lucy.

Craig shook his head. 'Sadly, there isn't.'

Lucy looked away so the others couldn't see her anguished face.

Joel switched off the engine, climbed out of the vehicle and peered at something on the ground. They watched as he walked a short way into the bush, still staring at the ground; then he came back and spoke in a low voice to Craig.

'Hang on a moment,' said Craig. He jumped off the roof, and he and Joel disappeared into the bush.

'What do you think it is, Ellie?' asked Kal.

'Something about tracks I think, but they were talking Maasai and I couldn't follow.'

The two men returned looking pensive. Craig climbed back onto the roof and they continued their drive.

The children looked at him, deep in thought.

'Were they some sort of tracks?' asked Kal.

'What? Oh yes; yes, they were… they were eland; we don't normally see eland in this area.'

Lucy glanced across at Ellie, who gave a slight shake of her head.

CHAPTER 6

Dik-dik

SEARCHING FOR DIAMONDS

They continued their journey in silence, climbing steadily, until they came onto a plateau that overlooked the plain below. Above them were forested hills with wispy clouds shrouding their summits. Craig called a final halt, and they clambered off the roof, feeling stiff after their bumpy ride.

'Thank goodness, we're still in one piece,' said Lucy.

'Let's have some lunch, take our mind off things,' said Craig. 'Over there, in the shade by that gully.'

They sat dangling their feet over the edge of the gully, while they munched sandwiches that Diana had prepared for them, and watched the birds coming to feed on the blossoms of an acacia tree on the opposite bank. Fupi sat close by, waiting to snap up any crumbs.

'These sandwiches are good,' said Lucy, 'what's in them?'

'*Kuku*, I guess,' said Craig.

'Cuckoo!'

'Yuk!' cried Kal, and spat out a mouthful. 'I'm not eating flaming cuckoo!'

'Don't be so pathetic,' said Ellie, 'don't you two know anything?'

'What's that supposed to mean?' said Lucy.

'*Kuku* is Swahili for chicken.'

'Oh,' said Lucy. 'Craig, why didn't you say?'

Craig chuckled. 'Eat up, guys, we need to make a move. Kal, can you drive the Landy?'

Kal grinned. 'Dunno, but I'll give it a go.'

'I'm not going in the Land Rover if Kal's driving,' said Lucy.

'Nor me,' said Ellie.

'Good, because I want you girls to go with Joel and do some geology,' said Craig.

'I don't know anything about geology,' grumbled Lucy.

Craig smiled. 'I don't know anything about geology either, that's why I've asked for your dad's help. But let's see if we can give him a start.'

'How?'

'You and Ellie, go with Joel. Look for places where stones have been washed out of the rock and settled in gullies, as well as collecting bits of exposed rock. That'll give your dad an idea of what's here.'

'Do you think we'll find diamonds?' asked Lucy.

'Lucy in the sky with diamonds,' said Craig. 'Dream on.'

Lucy grinned. What was wrong with dreaming?

Craig gave Joel a backpack in which to carry water, and plastic bags into which they could put the specimens. 'Either of you guys any good at maths?' he asked the girls.

'I'm useless,' said Lucy.

'Ellie?'

'All right,' she said cautiously.

'Have you seen one of these before?' Craig took something like a mobile phone out of a case.

Ellie shook her head.

'It's a GPS receiver.'

'A what?'

'A global positioning system receiver – it receives satellite signals and tells us where we are on the earth.'

'Our coordinates,' explained Kal.

'All right, Mr Know-All,' said Ellie.

'See, switch it on here,' said Craig, 'wait for a few seconds and then read off the numbers – as Kal says, the coordinates. Whenever you collect a sample, write down the details and put them in the bag with the samples. You reckon you can do that?'

'Yeah, no sweat,' said Ellie, grinning.

Craig gave her a playful punch on the shoulder.

'Right, on your bikes. See you later.'

Lucy and Ellie watched a nervous-looking Kal, sitting in the driving seat of the Land Rover listening to what Craig was saying. The engine started with a roar and a cloud of smoke shot out of the exhaust pipe. Then the engine stopped. A few moments later it started again (this time without the noise and smoke) and the vehicle edged jerkily forward. It reminded Lucy of the way her granny crossed the road. There was a call from Joel. The girls remembered their mission and joined him and Fupi, who were in a gully poking around in some stones.

They collected some brown stones, some black and white ones, and some greenish ones, but no diamonds. The stones didn't look very interesting but Lucy supposed that Dad would think they were. Ellie recorded the position. Lucy wrote it down on a piece of paper and put it in the bag. They followed the gully to its end, collecting as they went. When they emerged, they were on the edge of the forest. Lucy looked back. The Land Rover was now charging up and down the plateau flattening grass and bushes. Kal and machines!

Lucy tried to tell herself that they were doing scientific research; but if this was what science was all about, it was pretty boring. They'd now collected half a tonne of stones (which fortunately Joel was carrying) but they all looked dull and uninteresting. She had long given up any hope of finding diamonds.

Something shot out of a bush and ran off. Lucy jumped. Ellie squawked. Fupi stood quivering.

'What was that?' cried Lucy.

Joel pointed towards a bush about fifty paces away, and there was a most beautiful antelope – but it was tiny, no more than half a metre high. It was standing in the shade of the bush watching them with large eyes and whiffling a long soft nose in their direction.

'What is it, Joel?'

'*Diki diki.*'

'A dik-dik! It's beautiful.'

Fupi was like a coiled spring. Lucy knelt down beside her. 'Good girl.' Fupi jumped up and licked her face then transferred her attention back to the dik-dik, longing to go after it.

'And look – there's another,' whispered Ellie, pointing to the other side of the bush.

Joel nodded and smiled. They watched the two little antelopes for a while; then Joel looked at the sun. 'We must be returning,' he said.

'Wait!' cried Lucy. She dropped to her hands and knees, and peered at something on the ground. She picked it up. 'Look at that,' she breathed, passing a small piece of rock to Ellie.

Ellie held it up to the light. 'It's red,' she murmured. Her hand flew to her mouth. 'Ruby!'

'And here's another bit!' cried Lucy.

All three of them were now on their hands and knees, scrabbling and searching amongst the loose rocks. Fupi felt she too had to help and started digging furiously. When they stood up, they were covered in dust, their fingers were scratched and their nails broken, but they were grinning with delight.

'Brilliant!' cried Lucy.

'We must record the coordinates for Dad,' said Ellie, switching on the GPS monitor. She wrote down the figures. 'Let's go and show the others.'

They raced back to Craig and Kal.

'We've found rubies!' cried Lucy.

'What!' cried Craig. 'Let's see.'

They stared, spellbound, at the small heap of stones, all of which had bits of red embedded in them. Craig picked one up. 'I cannot believe it,' he murmured, 'and just lying on the surface?'

Lucy nodded. '*Is* it ruby?'

Craig examined another piece. 'We need your dad to confirm it, but it certainly looks like it to me.'

'The ranch is saved!' cried Lucy.

CHAPTER 7

Scorpion

THE CAMP IN THE FOREST

Ellie and Lucy had just finished putting up their tent. Lucy glanced round to make sure they were out of earshot. 'Did you make out any more about what Craig and Joel were discussing?' she whispered.

'What, when they went off into the bush together?'

'Yes.'

'Lucy, they weren't talking about eland – I'm sure they weren't. Joel told me the Maasai word for eland is *osiruwa*. I would have recognised it. I think they were talking about people.'

'What sort of people?'

'I'm not sure, possibly poachers.'

'Poachers!'

'Shh. Yes.'

'That could explain why they looked so serious.'

Ellie nodded.

'Could it be anything to do with the trouble that the policeman talked to Craig about, when we were at the hotel?'

Ellie shrugged. 'I don't know.'

Lucy frowned. 'Ellie, what's going on, and why won't Craig tell us about it?'

❧

Ellie had volunteered to be in charge of the food, and now they were sitting round a campfire watching her fry steak. Fupi was lying with her head on her paws, her nose twitching at the delicious smell.

Joel, who had been filling the Land Rover with petrol from jerry cans carried on the vehicle's roof, came and joined them.

'Aagh!' screamed Ellie, and leapt away from the fire nearly upsetting the frying pan. 'What's that?'

'Mind our supper!' cried Kal.

'It's only a scorpion,' said Craig.

'Only a scorpion!'

'Cool,' said Kal.

'He won't hurt you, as long as you leave him alone.'

'I might have been killed,' yelled Ellie.

'He could give you a nasty sting but it wouldn't be fatal.' Craig flicked the scorpion away with his boot. 'He was probably in one of the logs we put onto the fire.'

'Yikes!' yelled Kal, and leapt out of his seat. 'I've just been bitten!'

'*Siafu*,' murmured Joel.

'Yow!' yelled Kal, frantically brushing at his shorts. 'Jeepers! I'm being eaten alive!' He raced over to the Land Rover and leapt inside.

The others could hear him shouting and cursing. 'They're flaming ants! Yow! One's just bitten...'

Ellie joined in with the others who were roaring with laughter.

'It's all right for... Ouch!'

Craig hurried over to the Land Rover, found a tin of insect spray, and gave it to Kal. Then he came back and shone his torch on the ground. 'There, see. Watch where you put your feet.'

Lucy and Ellie looked at a line of brown treacle. Lucy peered closer. 'They *are* ants!' she cried. 'Millions of them!'

'*Siafu* – safari ants,' said Craig, 'Kal was unlucky enough to put his chair on top of their column.'

Joel moved their chairs to the other side of the fire.

'What happens if they come into the tents?' asked Ellie.

'They're heading away,' said Craig, 'we'll be okay.'

Ellie didn't look convinced. 'I'm keeping the insect spray with me.'

Kal reappeared, fully clothed. 'I could have been ruined for life,' he muttered.

'You do make a fuss,' said Lucy.

'It's all right for you,' retorted Kal, 'you didn't see the size of their jaws.'

'Okay, okay, so you got bitten by an ant.'

'I bet you'd make a fuss, if one latched onto *your* privates.'

'You'll live,' said Lucy.

Ellie was sitting on one of the chairs her feet tucked under her. 'You never told us we were all going to be eaten alive, Craig.'

'I don't think so.' Craig smiled. 'Ellie, let me tell you I'm far more scared in London than I ever am out here: all that traffic rushing about, the crush in the underground, and all those people – that frightens me.'

'That's different,' sniffed Ellie, 'there are no dangerous wild animals there.'

'People scare me more than animals. Besides, animals are only dangerous if you don't understand them.'

'Like Moshi?' said Lucy.

Craig shook his head. 'No, not like Moshi.'

'But she could have…'

'Sure, she was dangerous, but she behaved normally for an angry elephant. Why she is that way, *that's* what I don't understand.'

'Do you think she…'

'Hey, what's that?' Kal pointed at something fluttering in the light from the gas lamp.

Craig rose from his chair and caught the insect in his cupped hands. 'There's your ant-lion, Lucy.'

'It's beautiful; those lovely wings.' Lucy was fascinated. It really did look like a small dragonfly.

Kal and Ellie crowded round.

'That's really cool,' said Kal. Coming from him that was quite a compliment for something that wasn't mechanical.

Craig opened his hands and the insect fluttered off into the darkness.

'*Chakula tayari*,' called Joel. With all the excitement, they hadn't noticed that he had taken over the cooking.

'Food's ready,' said Craig.

Joel was serving up steaks with bread rolls, roasted sweet corn, tomatoes and bottles of cold drinks.

The children each took a plate and bottle and settled into their chairs.

'This is what picnics ought to be like,' said Lucy.

'Brirrmpph,' said Kal, his face stuffed with roll.

'Disgusting,' said Ellie.

'Brilliant,' repeated Kal, when he'd emptied his mouth.

After the meal, Ellie insisted on doing the washing up, and Kal did the drying-up – without being asked. Then they settled down round the fire, sipped their drinks straight from the bottle, and stared into the embers.

'You all right now, Ellie?' asked Craig.

She nodded. 'It just takes a while to get used to things.'

'Bit different from home in Putney,' said Kal.

Craig smiled. 'You guys are doing really well.'

They lapsed into silence for a while; then Joel got up. 'Good night,' he said, disappearing into the darkness.

'Good night,' they chorused.

'Where's Joel sleeping?' asked Lucy.

'On top of the Landy – he doesn't like tents,' said Craig.

'Can I sleep there?' asked Kal.

'No ways. I've put your tent there, next to the girls.'

'Where are you sleeping?'

Craig pointed to a camp bed with a mosquito net draped over it set on the far side of the clearing. 'I guess I'm like Joel, but I do find the roof of the Landy a bit too hard.' He rose and put another bit of wood on the fire.

'Isn't it brilliant about the rubies,' murmured Lucy.

'We mustn't get too excited until your dad confirms it,' said Craig.

'But he will. I just know he will.'

They sat staring into the fire. It was like being inside a magic bubble of flickering red and yellow light surrounded by darkness.

'Craig, can I ask you a question?' said Lucy, taking a sip from her bottle.

'Sure.'

She poked the fire with her foot and watched the sparks rise into the night and mingle with the stars. 'You remember when we stopped this morning, just before we got here?'

He nodded.

'You and Joel weren't talking about eland, were you?'

Craig looked up. 'Why do you say that?'

'Ellie says that Joel taught her the Maasai word for eland, and you didn't mention that. I think you were talking about people – about two men.'

'Hmm,' said Craig, turning back to stare into the fire.

'Was it two men?' asked Kal. 'Were they poachers?'

'I don't know.'

'What were they doing?'

'No way of knowing. All Joel could make out was the tracks of two men who had recently passed that way.'

'Could they have been poachers?' asked Kal.

'Possibly. But we haven't had trouble from poachers for a while.'

'Could it be linked to that trouble you and Reuben were talking about?' asked Ellie.

'Hey!' cried Craig, 'I really will have to watch what I say.'

'Who's Reuben?' asked Lucy.

'Who's Reuben!' cried Kal. 'He only won the Olympic...'

'He's that really good looking policeman we met at the hotel,' said Ellie.

'Oh, him,' said Lucy.

Craig smiled.

'*Could* it be linked, like Ellie says?' asked Kal.

'Possibly.'

'Tell us,' said Lucy.

'Okay, but keep it to yourselves.'

The children nodded.

Craig pushed a log into the fire with his boot. 'We've thought for some time there might be valuable minerals on the ranch and...'

'And now we've found them!' cried Lucy.

Craig smiled. 'It certainly looks like it. But unfortunately, other people have also heard about the minerals, and they'd like to get there first.'

'What sort of people?' asked Kal.

'Greedy people.'

'But this is your land,' said Ellie.

Craig nodded. 'Yes, but boundaries are difficult to define out here. We don't have any fences, and the only boundary markers are watercourses and tracks. It's very easy for people, if they want to make trouble, to dispute whose land is whose.'

'Is that why you spoke to Reuben?'

Craig nodded again. 'Yes, he's agreed to keep his ear to the ground.'

'Do you know who's making trouble?' asked Kal.

'I wish we did. Only a handful of people know about the possibility of the minerals.'

'Like who?'

'Samson and Joel know, but they wouldn't tell anyone. Some of the other men who work on the ranch may know a bit, but nothing much. And the management board; they oversee the running of the ranch – they had to approve my inviting your dad here. Then there's you lot. And that's about it.'

'You can trust us,' said Kal.

'I'm sure I can,' said Craig with a smile.

'Who's on the board?' asked Ellie.

'The Minister of Environment and Conservation – he's a good guy, a couple of neighbouring farmers, some Arusha businessmen, the local MP, the American Ambassador – she does a lot helping to raise US funds for us – and our solicitor James Msolla. I don't see any of them causing trouble.' Craig rose to his feet. 'Anyway, guys, enough of that; time for bed. Early start tomorrow.'

'Do we need to put the plates and things away?' asked Ellie.

'No, they'll be fine; just leave…' Craig's voice trailed off.

'What is it?' whispered Lucy.

He didn't reply. Fupi was also listening and whining quietly.

'Is there something out there?' whispered Lucy. 'It's not those two men?'

Craig turned back. 'No, no it's nothing. I was just imagining things.'

'Are you sure we're safe?' asked Ellie.

'No worries.' He scraped some sand over the fire to damp it down. 'See you in the morning.'

'Come on, Fupi,' said Lucy, and the little dog trotted after her. By the faint light of the moon, she saw Kal disappear into his tent. Then she looked back at Craig, and saw him take his rifle out of the back of the Land Rover before crossing to his camp bed. She followed Ellie into their tent, but didn't tell her about the rifle. Besides, Craig probably always kept it with him at night. She didn't bother to change into her pyjamas, but wriggled down into her sleeping bag. Fupi crawled in and snuggled against her. It was her first night in the African bush but she didn't feel afraid, despite what they had been talking about. She knew that Fupi would warn them if anything, or anyone, came in the night. And Joel was on the roof of the Land Rover, and Craig had his rifle – and they'd found rubies. Everything was just perfect. She was asleep.

CHAPTER 8

Tent in forest

ENCOUNTER IN THE FOREST

Ellie was still sound asleep when Lucy woke next morning. She unzipped the flap of the tent and peered out. Craig, Kal and Joel were sitting by the fire warming their hands on mugs of tea and chatting. Craig saw her and waved. She returned the wave; then slipped back into the tent. Her clothes from yesterday smelled of wood smoke, but having slept in them, she wasn't going to change them now. She put on her trainers, gave Fupi a hug, and joined the others by the fire.

'Sleep okay?' asked Craig.

'Like a log.'

'I knew you would.' He passed her a mug of tea. 'There you go.'

'Thanks.' She settled down beside them and let the magic of the cool morning wash over her. Apart from the occasional crackle from the fire, the only sounds were birdsong – no doors slamming, no people calling, no traffic noise, no radios blaring, no aeroplanes overhead. It was wonderful.

'What's that bird?' asked Lucy, pointing to the top of a large tree from which melodious whistling notes were coming.

'Black-headed oriole,' said Craig. 'Look, there it goes!'

Lucy caught sight of a flash of golden yellow as the bird flew to another tree and resumed its calling. 'What a beautiful call,' she said.

Craig smiled. 'Another one for your list, Lucy?'

She nodded.

'By the way,' said Craig, 'did you guys take a mug into the tent last night?'

'No.' Lucy shook her head. 'I don't think so. Why?'

'We had a visitor in the night.'

'What sort of visitor?'

'One that collects mugs.'

'Some animal?'

'They don't normally go off with mugs.'

'You mean a person?'

'Joel thinks so. He's found some tracks and is going to follow them up.'

'Can I go?' asked Kal.

'No ways. We're staying here. When he gets back, then we'll decide what to do.'

Kal and Lucy glanced at each other.

'Will it be safe?' asked Lucy. 'Sorry – I'm beginning to sound like Ellie.'

'Who is?' said a voice. And there was Ellie peering out of the tent and blinking like an owl in the early morning light.

'Nothing,' said Lucy.

'You were talking about me.'

'We were wondering how you could still be asleep on such a beautiful morning,' said Craig.

Ellie grunted and disappeared back into the tent.

'Craig, don't say anything about what's happened,' whispered Lucy, 'you know how worried Ellie can get.'

'Sure.' He turned and spoke to Joel, who went over to the Land Rover, pulled out a spear with a blade like a razor, and then disappeared into the forest.

Craig crossed to his camp bed and returned with his rifle, which he propped against a nearby tree.

They finished breakfast, and Ellie and Lucy had just taken down their tent, when they saw that Joel was back. Craig waved for the girls to join them. 'We're going hunting,' he said. 'You up for it?'

'What do you mean?' asked Ellie.

'You'll see. Just follow Joel, but don't get too close. I'll bring up the rear.' He fitted a lead to Fupi's collar; she looked most disapproving. 'There you go, Lucy.'

Lucy took Fupi's lead and tried to smile.

Craig picked up his rifle and nodded to Joel.

There was no time to feel afraid. They followed Joel along a narrow game trail into the forest: Kal first, then Lucy and Fupi, and then Ellie, who wanted to stay close to Craig at the rear. It was much cooler and darker here, and it took a while for their eyes to adjust to the gloom. They jogged gently downhill trying to be as quiet as possible. Lucy found the going was tiring, dodging round trees and ducking under branches. They came to a fork in the trail and Joel held up his hand. They stopped. Fupi was looking from one to other of them, her tail wagging uncertainly.

'We must be going slowly and be very quiet,' whispered Joel.

He crouched low and crept forward. The others followed. When they reached the top of a slope, they lay down and peered over. Joel pointed to what looked like a thick bush. He nodded to Craig, grasped his spear and began to advance. Kal was now almost on his heels, with Fupi just behind straining against the lead, and Lucy struggling to hold her back. Then Lucy realised it wasn't a bush; it was some sort of shelter.

Joel pointed with his spear at a heap of skins inside. It must be a poacher's den.

Lucy saw one of the skins move.

She put her hand over her mouth – too late to stop the scream.

Fupi barked.

The skins erupted and something leapt up.

Lucy saw two frightened eyes; then a skinny body shot out of the shelter. There was a tussle, and Joel hissed as a set of teeth sank into his arm. Then he was sitting on top of a dirty boy, pushing his face into the ground.

Fupi was still barking and it was all Lucy could do to hold her back.

Joel was now laughing despite the blood running down his arm. But the boy looked terrified.

'Who is it?' asked Ellie, sounding as if she'd got something stuck in her throat.

'Our night-time visitor, I suspect,' said Craig, coming out of the shelter with the missing mug and a bundle of wire snares.

Fupi was now growling and curling her lips.

'He's a poacher?' said Lucy

'Seems like it.'

'Look, over there!' cried Lucy. 'It's a dik-dik – like we saw yesterday.'

Craig went towards it. 'It's been tied up.'

'Is it a pet?' asked Lucy.

Joel muttered something.

'Joel thinks it's the boy's dinner,' said Craig.

'No!'

Craig untied the animal and carried it over to her. 'Lucy, I think one of its back legs is broken.'

'We can't leave it!' she cried.

'So what do we do? It's only a youngster, if we let him go he'll get chomped.'

'I'll look after him.'

'Are you sure, Lucy? It'll be a lot of work, and he may not survive.'

'I don't care. We must take him back.'

Craig sighed. 'Okay, another for the zoo, then.' He took Fupi's lead from Lucy and placed the baby dik-dik into her arms. It blinked its large round eyes and sniffed her clothes with its whiffly nose.

'Craig, he's so beautiful. I'm going to call him Caspar.'

'Why Caspar?'

'He's my pet cat – we had to leave him behind in England.'

'Why do you want to name him after that old rat bag?' said Kal.

'He's not a rat bag! The least we can do is remember him.'

Craig smiled. 'Caspar it is, then.' He turned to the boy who was now sitting up, but with his arms twisted behind his back by Joel. 'Now, my friend, what are we going to do with you?'

Fupi gave an extra growl as if to say: 'Think about that, Buster!'

Craig and Joel both tried talking to the boy, but he just stared ahead, apparently not hearing them. Suddenly, he began to shake and his eyes rolled up into his head. Fupi started barking again.

'Craig!' cried Ellie. 'He's sick. We must help him.' She grasped the boy's shoulders. His shaking subsided and his eyes came back into focus, but he still looked very frightened.

Joel spoke to him and pointed to Craig. The boy looked fearfully at Craig, who gave a savage growl, which Fupi repeated.

'Okay, Joel, let him go,' said Craig.

Joel hauled the boy to his feet. He looked to be about Kal's age, but he was terribly thin and dirty, and he had an open sore on his leg around which flies were feeding. Fupi sniffed it and the boy cringed away.

'Hey, what's this?' cried Kal, who had been poking around in the shelter and was now holding up a small bag made from the skin of some animal. The boy gave a cry, and would have rushed forward if Fupi hadn't growled.

'And look here,' said Kal. He was holding a small bow and some arrows.

'Don't touch those arrows!' shouted Craig.

Kal froze. 'What is it?'

'Let me see.'

Kal held out the arrows. The boy's eyes darted between him and Craig.

'Probably *Akocanthera*,' said Craig, looking at a sticky black paste smeared on their tips. 'It's a poison made from the roots of a bush that grows round here.' He dabbed a finger on the paste and cautiously licked it. 'Fresh. I guess there's enough poison on this arrow to kill an elephant.'

'Wicked,' murmured Kal, looking at the boy in awe, but now holding the arrows as though they were red-hot.

Joel took the arrows and wrapped them in one of the skins from the shelter.

'What's in the bag?' asked Craig.

'Just a few old stones.' Kal passed the bag over, and Craig tipped the stones onto his hand.

'They don't look very interesting,' said Ellie, 'like those we collected yesterday.'

'Well, let's see what your dad makes of them,' said Craig. He asked the boy a question, but he didn't answer.

⁓⊸⊚⊶⁓

When they were back at camp, Joel gave the boy some bread and a cup of milk. It was as though he hadn't eaten for ages. He relaxed a bit after he'd eaten, but still refused to answer any questions. He just stared ahead of him.

'What are we going to do with you?' said Craig, looking perplexed.

The boy continued to stare.

'Let me talk to him,' said Ellie. 'He's terrified of you two. He's convinced either you're going to shoot him or Joel is going to spear him.'

Craig frowned. 'I doubt you'll have much joy; he won't understand English and probably not much Swahili either.'

'That's all right, I'll try him in Maasai – Joel's been teaching me.'

Craig shook his head in disbelief.

While Ellie went to talk to the boy, Joel and Kal finished packing up the camp and loading the Land Rover, and Craig and Lucy examined Caspar. One of his back legs was floppy at the end. Craig felt it. 'It is broken,' he said, 'probably when he was caught in one of our friend's snares.'

'Will he be all right?'

'We should be able to fix it.'

Craig went to the Land Rover and came back with his medical box. He borrowed Joel's *simi* and cut two bits of stick from a nearby bush; then, with Lucy's help, bound the sticks against Caspar's leg with sticky tape, being careful not to make the dressing too tight. Caspar struggled but Lucy was sure he knew they were trying to help. When she told the little animal his

65

new name and what they were doing, he relaxed, and whiffled his nose and blinked his eyes.

Craig found an empty box in the back of the vehicle, and Lucy placed her sweater in the bottom and put Caspar on top. Then she collected some fresh leaves and offered them to him. He sniffed them suspiciously at first but then started to nibble. Lucy felt sure he was going to be all right.

'Don't forget he has to go back to the wild,' said Craig.

She gave a Sphinx-like smile but said nothing; then she whispered in Caspar's ear. He seemed to understand because he whiffled his nose again. It was a rubbery sort of nose that could bend round corners. Lucy thought it was really cute.

Craig went to join Ellie and the boy, who was eating another piece of bread.

'How's it going?' he asked.

'He won't tell me his name, Craig, but he says his home is over there.' She pointed into the distance. 'But he doesn't want to go back because he says he'll be beaten.'

'We can't just leave him here – besides that leg needs treatment.' Craig bent down and checked the wound. 'Hmm – not good.' He fetched his medical box and began to clean the wound.

'Ugh, that is so gross!' cried Ellie. She looked away and almost threw up. 'There are maggots in it!'

'They look horrible,' agreed Craig, 'but they probably helped to keep it free of infection.'

When Craig had finished, Joel helped the boy to get cleaned up and Kal gave him some spare clothes. Now he looked more cheerful and actually smiled.

'Okay, let's go,' said Craig, 'we're taking him home. Joel knows…'

'But he'll be beaten,' cried Ellie.

'I'm sorry, Ellie, he can't carry on living like that in the forest. It's the best thing for him.'

'Please, can't we…?'

'We've got to take him back.'

'But if…'

'Ellie, there's no alternative.'

'Why won't anyone listen to me?' She stormed off across the clearing and stared into the forest.

Craig winced. 'We're going, Ellie,' he called, 'let's get it over.'

Ellie made no move.

'We'll pick you up on the way home,' called Kal.

Ellie turned, ran back to the Land Rover, jumped inside and slammed the door. Lucy could see she'd been crying. She climbed in beside her sister and put her arm round her. 'Craig knows what he's doing,' she whispered. 'It really is the best.'

CHAPTER 9

Manyatta – Maasai settlement

LUCY SPEAKS HER MIND

Ellie and Kal sat with the boy between them, and Lucy sat in the back of the Land Rover making sure Caspar didn't jump out of his box. They drove mostly in silence, although Ellie (with some help from Joel) kept talking quietly to the boy.

They picked up a track about half an hour after leaving their campsite, and continued driving on it for nearly an hour before coming to a fork.

'We're going left here,' said Craig, 'this is where we leave the ranch.'

Soon after, a settlement came into view, which Joel said was called a *manyatta*. It consisted of a circle of low huts made out of sticks and skins, which he said the women covered in cow dung when the rains came.

'Why do women get all the rubbish jobs?' muttered Lucy.

'It's because… Ouch!' cried Kal, as Lucy prodded him from behind.

There was an untidy broken fence of thorn branches round the shabby huts, and the only thing that looked new was a shiny vehicle parked under a nearby tree. Some women were sitting on the ground scraping a cow skin, while some scruffy children with flies over their faces, crawled amongst them. The whole place looked really sad, and Lucy had an uneasy feeling that something was very wrong. She wasn't surprised that the boy looked unhappy – in fact, he looked terrified.

Craig switched off the engine. Some dogs barked, their hackles rose, and they began to walk towards the vehicle on stiff legs. Fupi glared at them and growled. Joel put his head out of the window and called to the women. They looked up without showing any interest; then one of them rose and went into the nearest hut. Joel got out of the vehicle and waited.

'What's happening?' asked Lucy.

'Joel has asked to see the owner of the *manyatta* – a man called ole Tisip,' said Craig. 'I don't know the guy, but Joel says he's bad news.'

'The place looks a bit rundown.'

'I'm surprised. The Maasai people normally keep their *manyattas* very tidy.'

'I said we shouldn't have come here, but no one listened,' muttered Ellie.

'I've seen that Range Rover before,' said Kal, staring at the vehicle. 'I'm sure it's the one. It was at the hotel, the day we arrived.'

'There are plenty of Range Rovers around nowadays,' said Craig.

'Yeah, but I bet there aren't too many silver V8 supercharged Vogue SEs like that.'

'True.'

'The reason I noticed it, was there were these two dodgy guys standing nearby; I thought they were going to try and nick it. But then the owner came out and they all went off together, with one of the guys driving.'

'Could it have been a hijack?' asked Craig, 'that sometimes happens.'

'I don't think so; the owner seemed to know them.'

'Are you sure you didn't imagine it?' said Lucy.

'No, I didn't! The owner was short and… That's him! That's Toad Face!'

Two men had emerged from the hut. One of them was tall and skinny, and wearing a dirty brown blanket, Wellington boots and a woolly hat. The other was rather fat and wearing a suit.

'That *is* him!' cried Kal. 'The one in the suit – I'm sure it's him.'

'Good grief,' muttered Craig. 'It's Gideon Nagu, our local MP. What did you call him?'

'Toad Face.'

'Suits him,' said Lucy.

'Didn't you say he was on Simba's management board?' said Ellie.

Craig nodded.

'But what's he doing here?'

'I've no idea,' said Craig. 'Kal, is the other guy one of the men you saw at the hotel?'

'No, I don't think so.'

The two men looked suspiciously at the visitors; then began to walk towards the Land Rover.

'Hang onto Fupi,' said Craig, getting down from the vehicle, 'and stay here.'

The boy didn't need any encouragement – he was cowering on the floor.

'*Jambo*, Craig,' cried Toad Face, a phoney smile on his face.

'*Jambo*, Gideon,' said Craig, as he shook the man's hand. 'How are you?'

'Fine, fine.'

'What brings you here?'

'Just a social call – you know how it is. Just meeting my old friend, ole Tisip.'

The other man said nothing and made no attempt to offer his hand.

'What's that thing the tall man's holding?' whispered Lucy.

'It's called a *rungu*; it's a kind of club,' whispered Ellie.

'I bet that could do some damage,' muttered Kal.

'So, my friend,' said Toad Face, putting an arm round Craig's shoulder, 'is yours also a social call?'

Craig said something that the children couldn't hear, and the tall man started shouting and waving his arms.

The boy cowered even further down on the floor.

'Can you understand what he's saying, Ellie?' whispered Lucy.

'He's talking about the boy.'

'Shouting about him, more like – what's he saying?'

'He's saying the boy is bad. He seems to be blaming him for the fact that cows have been dying, and that's why his place is in such a mess.'

'That's not fair,' said Lucy, 'and Craig certainly doesn't think so.' She could see he had his arms folded across his body and his mouth shut tight, as the man ranted on.

'Craig has told him he's sick and needs treatment. Hang on – that tall man said something about being the best thing if he died.'

'How dare he say that!' And before Ellie could stop her, Lucy

71

jumped down from the vehicle and ran over to the men. Fortunately, Kal was holding Fupi's collar or she would have followed.

'He needs help – he's sick!' Lucy stormed. 'You can't say he should be left to die!'

The man couldn't have been more surprised than if she'd just teleported from Planet Zorg. His mouth dropped open, showing stained brown teeth, and he was dribbling.

'I think you're horrible!' she yelled. 'And if I was him, this is the last place on earth I would want to live!'

The man clearly didn't understand a word she was saying, but Toad Face did, and he looked just as startled.

'Well, well, who's this?' he managed to say.

Lucy thought he had a silly squeaky voice, and she noticed his smile had gone. She didn't like the look that replaced it.

'I'm his friend,' she shouted. She could feel tears starting in the back of her eyes, but she wasn't going to let *them* see. 'And he's coming home with us!'

'Come on, Lucy, let's go,' said Craig, putting his arm round her. He turned and said something to the two men, and led her back to the Land Rover. Joel followed.

⁓❦⁓

Lucy sat in the front between Craig and Joel with Fupi on her lap. No one said anything as they drove away from the *manyatta*.

Then Craig said in a quiet voice: 'That was very brave, Lucy – I was proud of you.'

She couldn't hold back the tears any longer.

'Lucy, you were brilliant,' said Ellie. Then *she* started.

Craig stopped the vehicle and got out his hankie.

'I'm so sorry,' Lucy sniffled, as Fupi licked her face. 'Craig, I didn't mean to cause trouble; I was so…'

'You've probably just saved the boy's life.'

Lucy sat up – the tears forgotten. 'What?'

'It seems that his parents are both dead…'

'He's an orphan?'

Craig nodded. 'Yes, and no one was prepared to look after him.'

'That's awful!'

'So, without treatment, he would probably have died there, or more likely run away again and died in the bush.'

'Can't he stay… I mean can he come with…?' She couldn't say the words.

'Can he come with us?'

'Yes – that is…'

'I was about to tell ole Tisip what I'd decided, when you, young lady, arrived on the scene and expressed rather more forcefully what I was about to say.'

'So he *can* stay with us?'

Craig nodded. 'For a while, anyway.'

'Yes!'

'Is he going to be okay?' asked Kal.

'That leg needs treating, but I reckon we can do that back home; if not, I'll take him to the hospital at Shinyanga.'

The boy was now sitting up trying to follow their conversation. He couldn't understand what they were saying but he knew they were talking about him. Then Joel explained, and he looked very pleased. Lucy grinned at him, and he gave an uneasy smile.

'He reminds me of the ant-lion,' said Ellie suddenly.

'Oh yeah,' said Kal.

'It's true. Before, he was hunting and hiding in that dark place in the forest, and now he has come out into the open, like into a new life – just like the ant-lion.'

'What a load of rubbish,' said Kal.

'No – think about it.'

Joel was laughing.

'Why do you think that's funny, Joel?'

Joel made snapping movements with his fingers and pointed to the wound on his arm. 'That one has the teeth.'

'He's got to tell us his name now, Joel,' cried Lucy.

Joel turned and spoke to the boy, then chuckled. 'He says is name is Matata.'

'What does that mean?'

'It means trouble; it's what his mother used to call him.'

'What's his real name?'

'It is a difficult Maasai name – even for me.'

'Matata it is, then,' cried Craig.

'Just like the song from "Lion King!"' cried Ellie. '*Hakuna matata* – no worries, no problem.'

'Let's hope so,' said Craig, grinning.

Ellie and Lucy began to sing, until there was a sudden shout from Kal. 'Caspar's escaped!'

'Craig, stop!' yelled Lucy. She jumped out and ran round to the back door of the Land Rover. Caspar had climbed out of his box and managed to get himself stuck between two bags. She lifted him clear, and he whiffled his nose as if to say thank you.

❧

They returned to Craig's plane and, while he and Kal flew back, Joel drove the rest of them to the Simba house.

When they arrived, Craig handed Matata over to Martha, who made a great fuss of him and took him to her own house.

Lucy helped Craig remove the temporary splint from Caspar's leg, which they set in plaster. Then they put him in the pen with a baby eland. Although the two were very different in size, they sniffed each other's noses and immediately became friends. Lucy could see the eland, whose name was Pofu, was explaining to Caspar everything that went on at Simba. Afterwards, Caspar found himself a quiet corner in the pen and sat with his eyes half-closed pretending to be asleep. He didn't seem at all frightened; it was as if he'd always lived there.

⁂

That evening, just after they'd finished dinner on the veranda, Martha appeared, twisting her apron in her hands. 'Please, Diana, it's the boy, Matata.'

'What's the matter with him?'

'Has he run away?' cried Lucy.

Martha shook her head. 'No. It's just that… it's…'

'What, Martha?' asked Diana.

'God has told me I won't have any children of my own and…' Her apron twisting became more agitated.

'Go on, Martha,' said Diana.

'Now Matata has come… and he has no home … and I… that is Samson and me, we could look after him… and he could live with us… and we could feed him … and he wouldn't be any trouble… and we would make sure he was a good boy… that is if…' She was now looking at her feet, but still working her apron. 'Would you and Craigi let Matata stay with us?'

Diana glanced at Craig and then at Martha. Ellie, Kal and Lucy looked at each other, not daring to say a word.

'Does he not have any family?' asked Diana.

'His parents are both dead,' said Martha. 'He had a sister but she died. That man, ole Tisip, wouldn't pay for her to get medicine.'

'He's so awful!' cried Lucy.

'Have you said anything to the boy?' asked Diana.

Martha nodded still looking at her feet. 'He would be very

75

happy. He says the *wazungu* children and Craigi are very kind.'

'What does Samson say?'

'He says that it is God who has brought Matata to us.'

Diana sat thinking for a moment. 'Well,' she said slowly, 'we could do with some help with the orphan animals when Lucy leaves, and...'

'Yes!' yelled Lucy, leaping up and giving Diana a huge kiss. She looked rather startled.

Ellie and Kal were grinning.

'I'm sure he'll be very happy with you,' said Diana.

Martha used her apron to wipe her eyes and looked up with a big smile. 'That's brill.'

'That's what?' said Diana.

'That's brill,' said Martha, looking uncertain.

'Where on earth did you learn that word?'

Martha turned to Lucy, who had gone bright red. 'From Lucy.'

'I see.' Diana paused. 'Well, I suppose it is rather brill.'

Everyone laughed.

'An orphan to help with the orphans,' said Craig, 'sounds good to me.'

'Splendid.' Diana smiled. 'Why not bring him through, Martha?'

A few moments later Martha returned with Matata. He was looking squeaky clean and very nervous – and he was wearing Kal's England football shirt.

'Kal, that's your favourite shirt!' whispered Lucy.

'But I've got loads of football shirts – he hasn't got any,' said Kal, looking embarrassed.

CHAPTER 10

Open Land Rover

A DANGEROUS CONFRONTATION

At the end of the week, Craig flew down to Arusha to collect Mum and Dad. He buzzed low over the house to announce their return.

Kal yelled to Lucy and Ellie when he heard the plane, and the three of them piled into the open Land Rover, which Kal was now allowed to drive, and sped off to the airstrip.

Craig taxied to meet the waiting vehicle, and as soon as he switched off the engine and opened the door, the children rushed forward.

'Mum, we've found rubies, and the ranch is going to be...'

'And Craig and I have been flying...'

'And I've got this beautiful little dik-dik – it's a kind of antelope – he's called...'

'And we rescued this boy called Matata, but that's not his real…'

'And Craig says we can…'

'It's so lovely to see you all,' cried Mum, hugging them each in turn. 'Just look at you!'

With all the time they'd spent in the open, Kal's hair was getting bleached, Ellie's spots had disappeared, Lucy's nose was peeling because she always forgot to put sun cream on it, and all of them were tanned. 'You look so well!'

Dad arrived, carrying his briefcase. 'How are you kids?' he asked. 'Having a good time?'

'Yes thanks, Dad,' they chorused.

'Dad,' cried Lucy, 'we've found some rubies!'

'Really?' said Dad. 'That is good news.'

They looked up at the sound of another vehicle arriving. Joel was driving, and Matata and Fupi were with him.

'The driver is Joel and that's Matata – the boy we rescued,' said Ellie.

'Yes, dear,' said Mum. 'He's wearing a shirt just like Kal's.'

Ellie quickly explained.

'Kal, that's really generous.'

'No sweat.'

Lucy noticed Mum give a slight start. Kal was sounding more like Craig by the minute. He'd told Lucy that he wasn't trying to copy Craig's accent, it just happened that way. She didn't believe him.

Craig called to Kal: 'Go and teach Matata to play football.' He pulled out a new football that he had bought that morning in Arusha and booted it across to Kal, who skilfully trapped it, then flicked it onto his head and bounced it a few times. Matata watched in amazement.

'Here, Mat.' Kal kicked the ball across. Matata stopped it with his foot and kicked it towards Kal, but it spun off his toe and shot off to the side.

'Like this,' called Kal. He demonstrated, and Matata returned a perfect pass.

'Shouldn't we be getting on?' said Dad. 'Work to do.'

'Yes, sure,' said Craig. 'Okay, guys, bring the ball back; you can practise on the lawn.' He turned to Dad. 'David, would you mind going with Joel and Matata, the rest of us will go in the other vehicle.'

'You're not letting Kal drive, I hope,' said Mum, as they climbed aboard.

'Why not?'

'Well I... he's not... he doesn't...' She was floundering. 'He hasn't passed his test.'

'He has with me.'

'But shouldn't you be sitting beside him?'

'Why?'

'Well... in case he...'

'In case he what?' Craig was smiling.

'In case... Nothing!' Mum grinned. 'Come on, Kal, what are we waiting for?' She turned to the girls: 'Isn't this wonderful.'

'Mum, it's just brilliant,' cried Lucy.

The track emerged from the trees, and the house lay in front of them.

'Mum, see all the birds,' said Lucy, 'those orange and blue ones making all that noise are superb starlings, and there's a scarlet-chested sunbird (or maybe a Hunter's sunbird, they're very similar), and those ones on the lawn are hoopoes, and those are masked weavers, and...'

'Lucy, Lucy,' cried Mum, 'I can't take it all in.'

'Craig's been teaching me the names of all the different birds – I'm making a list and I've already recorded over a hundred.'

'That's marvellous.'

Kal pulled up, and Diana came forward and embraced Mum. 'Lovely to see you again, Sarah, after all these years – how long has it been?'

'Must be fifteen at least,' said Mum to her aunt, 'certainly before the children were born.'

'My, how time flies.' Diana led the way up the steps of the veranda. 'Welcome to Simba.'

'Grab some seats,' said Craig, pushing some chairs forward after the various animals on them had been shooed off.

'Nice spot this, Craig,' said Dad. 'I was studying the geology as we flew in. It appears that the main formations are pre-Cambrian with volcanic intrusions – they're probably quaternary.'

'That's what I thought,' murmured Kal, glancing at Lucy and Ellie, who started giggling.

Dad ignored them. 'I imagine you still have some seismic activity in the area.'

'We get the occasional earth tremor, but nothing serious,' said Craig.

'Rock falls – that kind of thing?'

'Yes, and once the kitchen door jammed.'

Dad nodded. 'I would expect that. Now,' he continued, 'the main areas of interest from a mineral perspective will probably be at the margins where intrusions have pushed up through the basement rock.'

'Exactly,' murmured Kal, his hand over his mouth.

Craig winked at him, and tried to follow what Dad was saying.

'Take those hills there, for example,' said Dad, pointing into the distance, 'they could be a promising place to start.'

'Those are the Seki Hills,' cried Lucy, 'where we found the rubies. Ellie's recorded the coordinates on Craig's GPS – that's a global positioning system.'

'Yes, Lucy, I am familiar with the technology.'

'Oh. I just thought… '

There was a rattle of crockery, and Diana and Ellie appeared carrying the lunch trays.

'Come and sit down, everyone,' called Diana.

'So, Craig, what's the plan?' asked Dad, as soon as they were settled.

'I thought we'd spend today here, then tomorrow fly over the Seki Hills and other parts of the ranch, and you can decide what you want to look at from the ground.'

Dad nodded. 'Good.'

'Sarah, would you like to come?' asked Craig.

'I'd love to.'

'Kal?'

'Yeah, sure.'

'But you'd better not do the flying tomorrow,' whispered Craig, 'your parents might get worried.'

Kal nodded.

'In the meantime, Craig,' Dad was saying, 'perhaps I could examine the samples you've collected. Did Lucy say something about rubies?'

'I'll go and get them,' cried Lucy.

As soon as the lunch table was cleared and the others were having coffee, Dad extracted a field microscope from his briefcase and began examining the rocks.

Lucy was sitting on the edge of her seat trying to keep still. 'Are they rubies, Dad?'

'Lucy do be patient,' said Mum.

'Yes, but are they rubies?'

Dad looked up. 'No, Lucy. I'm sorry to say they're not rubies.'

'Not rubies! But those red...'

'They are garnets.'

'What are *they*?' Lucy slumped back in her chair. 'So much for research!' she muttered.

'A form of calcium or magnesium aluminium silicate – probably common in the area. But what I find so interesting is...'

'Are they valuable?' asked Kal.

'They have some trivial value.' Dad waved a dismissive hand.

The children sat looking dejectedly at each other.

Craig got up. 'Anyone for more coffee?'

They all shook their heads.

'I guess it's back to the drawing board, then,' said Craig.

⚬⊰⊱⚬

Mum had been to her *banda* and changed, and was now back on the veranda. Craig and Dad were examining the other rocks that had been collected, Kal and Matata were playing football, and Diana had gone into the house to talk to Martha about dinner. So Ellie and Lucy pounced on Mum and started to tell her everything that had happened. They were just getting to the bit about the *manyatta*, when Kal came racing up the steps looking hot.

'That man's come,' he cried.

'What man?' asked Craig.

'Toad Face.'

'Do you mean, Gideon Nagu?'

'Yeah, if that's his name. He wants to talk to you, Craig.'

'Where's Matata?' asked Ellie.

'He legged it as soon as he saw who it was,' said Kal.

'Who is this person you're talking about?' asked Dad.

'He's horrible!' said Lucy. 'He's all podgy and has a really creepy voice.'

'His name is Gideon Nagu,' said Craig, 'he's a member of our management board, and also happens to be our local MP.'

'Really, you two,' said Dad, 'you should be more respectful. This is a good opportunity to meet him. It's important to be on good terms with such people.'

'Dad, he's a creep,' Lucy muttered.

'Lucy, that's quite enough!' said Mum.

'Ah, Craig my friend.'

Lucy immediately recognised the squeaky voice, and turned to see the man come puffing up the steps of the veranda.

'Good afternoon, Gideon,' said Craig, getting to his feet. The two men shook hands. Fupi growled and Toad Face looked uncertainly at her.

'Is that one safe?' he asked.

'As long as I'm here,' said Craig.

The man backed away.

Dad hurried forward. 'Good afternoon, sir, I'm Doctor David Bartlett; Craig has called me in as a geology consultant. I'm very pleased to have this opportunity to meet you.' He shook the man's podgy hand.

The man looked a bit surprised but quickly put on his phoney smile.

'Good afternoon, doctor. Are you enjoying your visit?'

'Yes, very much. I've only just arrived, but I have reason to think there could be some promising mineral deposits in those hills over there.' He pointed in the direction of the Seki Hills.

'Is that so – promising in what way?'

'Well, I haven't had a chance to see things from the ground but aerial inspection suggests that…'

'David,' interrupted Craig, 'I don't think we should raise expectations at this stage – not until you've had a chance to visit the site.'

'No, perhaps you're right.' Dad turned back to the man. 'I do apologise, sir, my enthusiasm sometimes gets the better of me.'

'Please don't apologise – what you tell me, doctor, sounds most interesting. Those hills, you say?'

'Actually, Gideon,' said Craig, 'Dr Bartlett and I must have been talking at cross-purposes. The material came from that escarpment.' He pointed in a different direction.

'But I thought you said it was from…'

'Can I offer you some tea or coffee, Gideon?' asked Craig.

'No, I won't stay; I just came about that boy.'

'What boy?'

'The boy you brought to my friend's *manyatta* the other day, when you were with the charming English children – so spirited.'

'Creep,' muttered Lucy.

'What about him?' said Craig.

'My friend ole Tisip apologises that there was a misunderstanding; he will be very happy to look after the boy. So, I've come to take him back.'

'You can't!' cried Lucy.

'Charming, charming,' murmured the man.

'No, Gideon,' said Craig quietly, 'he is happy here.'

Lucy wanted to rush up and hug Craig.

'But this is not his home.'

'It is now.'

'Craig, we should discuss this. It would be better for the boy to grow up in his traditional environment.'

'Sorry, Gideon, there is nothing to discuss.'

'I'm only thinking what is best for the boy.' The phoney smile was disappearing fast.

'So am I, Gideon – he stays.'

'I think you're being very short-sighted,' snapped the man.

'Gideon, the boy stays here. He's being cared for by my assistant manager and his wife.'

'You, my friend, are being very foolish.' He glared at Craig; then turned, went down the steps, climbed into his vehicle and drove off.

'What a dreadful man,' said Mum.

'He was perhaps a bit forceful,' conceded Dad. 'But I respect that in a man.'

'Dad!' cried Lucy.

'Do you think he'll make trouble?' asked Mum.

'No.' Craig shook his head. 'I know he's on the board, but he's not as important as he thinks.'

But Lucy could tell he was just saying that so Mum wouldn't be worried.

Craig turned to Dad. 'David, I apologise for interrupting you, but I think the fewer people who know about things the better at this stage.'

'Absolutely. But the man *is* an MP.'

Craig nodded. 'Yes, but he has some rather dodgy friends.'

CHAPTER 11

Dad's microscope

THE SKIN BAG

'Dad,' asked Ellie, when they had recovered from the unwelcome visit, 'apart from garnets, what else did we find in the hills?'

Dad's eyes lit up. 'Well, the more interesting samples are probably metasomatic with corundum and hornblende inclusions – possibly zoizite...'

'You what?' said Kal.

'Let me finish! Zoizite, or zoizite-amphibolite, occurs in metasomatic rocks, schists and gneisses. These probably comprise the more interesting components of those hills.'

'Interesting!' muttered Kal.

Dad gave him a withering look. 'A form of zoizite, known as tanzanite, gets its name from this country.'

'I've heard of that,' said Craig.

'Tanzanite has some trifling value like garnet,' continued Dad, 'but what may be significant are the traces of corundum.'

'Grinding powder?' said Craig.

'Exactly.'

'Grinding powder! And that's it?' said Lucy.

'Yes, Lucy, that is it. Geologically, though, the samples are extremely interesting, and I look forward to examining the area tomorrow, but in terms of valuable deposits, I fear we may be disappointed.'

'What about the stones that Matata had in his bag?' asked Kal.

'No!' Craig clapped his hand to his forehead. 'I forgot all about them.'

'Craig, you didn't leave them!' cried Lucy.

'No ways, they're in the door of the Landy.'

'I know,' said Kal. He raced off and was back a few minutes later with the skin bag. Craig opened it and tipped out the contents.

'Hmm,' said Dad, 'now these *do* look interesting – probably from alluvial deposits.'

'What are loovile deposits?' asked Lucy.

'Alluvial. Really, the ignorance of this family!' Dad gave a deep sigh. 'It's where stones are washed out by water and get deposited in hollows and gullies.' He picked up one of the stones and set it under his microscope. He adjusted the light and turned the stone round using different lenses and different lighting arrangements to examine it, and began humming tunelessly to himself.

'What is it, Dad?' asked Ellie.

Dad didn't hear her. He picked up another stone and carried on humming. He examined five more stones, and when he finally looked up his eyes were shining.

'I'm pretty certain they contain trigonal prismatic forms of corundum.'

'More grinding powder, then?' said Kal.

'In the granular form, yes, but in the form we have here, it is better known as ruby.'

Kal said a word, that had Mrs Sandford heard it she would have had had him in detention for a week. They were all so stunned that not even Mum thought of telling him off. For a moment, there was complete silence; then they all started to talk at once.

'So we are rich and...'

'Do you think Matata knows what they...?'

'David, are you sure...?'

 'Can we go back there and...?'

'Good heavens, what's going on?' Diana had emerged from inside the house. 'You look as though you've just seen a ghost or something.'

'Diana, it's rubies – you're going to be rich!' cried Lucy.

'How nice, dear.'

'Mother, it's true,' said Craig, 'David says that some of the stones Matata had contain traces of ruby.'

'Possibly sapphire as well,' added Dad.

'Good Lord!' Diana had to sit down.

'Probably of gem quality,' said Dad, 'but I would need a second opinion to be sure – someone like Professor Wafula at the University of Nairobi in Kenya would know.'

'Dad, I thought sapphires and rubies were different,' said Ellie.

'Sapphire and ruby are both forms of corundum,' said Dad, 'but they contain different colouring pigments: normally chrome for ruby, and iron and titanium for sapphires, the colouring depends on...'

'Not another geology lecture,' groaned Kal.

Dad scowled.

'And these stones were found on the ranch?' said Diana.

'We need to ask Matata,' said Craig, 'but I'm assuming they were.'

'No wonder old Toad Face was interested,' said Lucy.

'Who?' asked Diana.

'Lucy means our local MP,' said Craig.

Diana raised her eyebrows. 'I thought I heard a vehicle. What did he want?'

'He wanted to take Matata away.'

'Whatever for?'

'He said he thought it would be best if he grew up in his traditional environment. But I told him that Matata is staying.'

'He looked livid,' said Lucy.

'Craig, do you think he knew Matata had those stones with him?' asked Ellie.

'Could be,' said Craig, 'but one thing's for sure, he wasn't interested in Matata's welfare. He was...' He stopped. 'I think it's time I had another word with Reuben. But first I'll talk to Matata, and find out where he found the stones.'

'No,' said Ellie. 'Let me talk to him; you'll frighten him – he'll think he's done something wrong.'

'Fair enough.'

Ellie stood up. 'Kal, do you want to come?'

'I won't be much help, I can't understand much of what he says.'

'No, but you're his friend, he'll be more relaxed if you're there.'

Fupi, sensing something was about to happen, jumped off Lucy's lap and ran after them.

◦≈⊚≈◦

'It took us ages to find Matata,' said Kal, when he and Ellie returned. 'In the end, it was Fupi who found him hiding in some bushes. He thought Toad Face had come to take him away.'

'He was right, there,' said Lucy, 'but what did he say about the stones?'

'At first he pretended he didn't understand what I was talking about,' said Ellie, 'but then I said that the fat man knew about the stones and had come to take them.'

'What did he say to that?' asked Craig.

'He got very frightened and said his father had given them to him to look after.'

'His father! Did he say why?'

'He said his father was afraid, that's why he gave him the stones.'

'And soon after that his father died,' said Craig. 'Do you know how he died?'

'I didn't ask.'

'Does Matata know where the stones came from?' asked Lucy.

'He tried to tell me but I couldn't really understand what he was saying,' said Ellie. 'It sounded like *mahali pa mfupi ya kichwa*; which sort of means "the Place of the Short of the Head", but that doesn't make sense.'

'Soft in the head, if you ask me,' said Kal.

'Are you sure you got it right, Ellie?' said Lucy.

'I made him repeat it several times; then he got all upset, so I had to stop.'

'What does it mean, Craig?' asked Kal.

'More or less what Ellie says, but there must be something else to it.' Craig frowned. 'I wonder what.'

Lucy tried to think. It was like when Mrs Sandford asked her difficult sums such as the square root of eighty one, or what was seven by nine. She knew she knew the answers, but they got stuck in a jumble of numbers and she could never find the right one. 'Think,' she whispered to Fupi, sitting on her lap. Fupi wagged her tail and Lucy could tell she was thinking because her brows seemed to furrow. 'Think, Fupi,' she urged.

The others looked perplexedly from one to another.

'Got it!' cried Lucy, leaping up.

Fupi fell onto the floor with a bump, then jumped up and ran round barking "*Eureka*", or whatever it is that dogs say when they've made a great discovery.

'Tell us, Lucy,' said Mum.

'There's your answer,' cried Lucy, pointing at Fupi.

'I told you it meant soft in the head,' muttered Kal.

'No, listen. Ellie, tell us again what Matata said.'

'It sounded like: *mahali pa mfupi ya kichwa*.'

'And you said it meant the "Place of the Short of the Head?"'

Ellie nodded.

'The *mfupi* bit means short. Right?'

'Yes.'

'And Fupi's called *mfupi*, because she's short.'

'*I* told you that,' said Kal.

'All right, but Craig told *you*.'

'Lucy, that's it!' cried Ellie, 'the Place of Fupi's Head. Just like that's called *Mlima ya Simba* – Lion Hill.' She pointed to the hill overlooking the house. 'This is a place where there's a rock or hill or something, that's shaped like Fupi's head.'

'Exactly!' cried Lucy. 'Fupi, you are clever, having a place named after you.'

'Well *done*, you two,' cried Mum.

But Craig shook his head. 'Sorry, guys, that won't wash.'

'Why?' said Kal.

'Remember, Matata never met Fupi before he came to us, and it's almost certain that his father didn't. So, there's no way that the father would name a place after a dog he'd never met.'

'Oh,' said Lucy, feeling deflated. 'I thought we'd solved the mystery.'

'I think we *have* solved it, but not quite as you've suggested. I think it's something rather more sinister.'

Mum and Ellie exchanged anxious glances.

'Ellie,' said Craig, 'you said you couldn't be sure you'd heard Matata correctly. Could he have said: *mahali pa mfupa ya kichwa*?'

'What's the difference?' asked Lucy.

'*Mfupi* means short; but *mfupa* means bone.'

'The Place of the Bone of the Head,' said Lucy slowly.

'I think so. And what's that?'

Lucy thought hard, and this time it came. 'The skull!' she cried. 'The Place of the Skull!'

'I guess so.'

The children looked uneasily at each other.

'Do you know where it is, Craig,' asked Mum.

'No, I've never heard of it.'

'Ellie, does Matata know?' asked Lucy.

'No, his father told him about the place but never took him there, but I think it's somewhere in those hills where we found him.'

'The Seki Hills,' said Craig. 'Could be.'

'Where we're going tomorrow?' said Mum.

Craig nodded.

'I'm glad I'm not coming,' said Ellie.

CHAPTER 12

Saw-scaled viper

DISASTER

Dad had hardly finished breakfast next morning before he was pacing up and down, saying things like: 'long day ahead of us,' and, 'we don't want to leave it too late.' He already had his briefcase with him and was looking at his watch.

There was the sound of a vehicle and Joel drove up in the Land Rover.

Dad, Mum, Craig and Kal piled in, and Joel drove them down to the airstrip.

Twenty minutes later, they were airborne and Craig flew back and forth over the Seki Hills, while Dad peered out of the window, consulting his GPS, making notes, and taking photographs. After a while, he tapped Craig on the shoulder.

'I've seen enough from the air,' he shouted.

Craig nodded and turned towards their new airstrip.

Soon after a rather bumpy landing, they were in the shade of the wing, sipping cold drinks from the cool box that Craig had brought, and watching Dad lay out some aerial photographs on the ground.

'These are the photos you and Kal took,' he said. 'I was studying them last night.'

'We're about here,' said Craig, pointing to one of the photographs.

Dad made a mark. 'How far away are these places? I'd like to start with them.' He pointed at crosses he had made earlier.

'That one's probably about a mile and a half,' said Craig, 'the other, a bit further.'

'We should be getting along, then.'

'You guys, okay, or do you want to wait here?' asked Craig, turning to Mum and Kal.

'It's lovely being in the open,' she said. 'I'm coming.'

'Me too,' said Kal.

Craig put the cool box back in the plane, and returned carrying a rucksack and his rifle. He must have seen Mum's nervous look. 'Just in case, Sarah – we might meet a lion or a buffalo.'

'Or an elephant,' murmured Kal.

❧❧❧

Two hours later, they finished their survey of the first spot marked on the photograph. Dad had collected several samples, but was clearly not finding anything of interest.

'A bit disappointing,' he said. 'Can we move on?'

'Let's have a break first,' said Craig, setting down his rifle and rucksack in the shade of a tree.

'What a beautiful spot,' said Mum.

There was a sudden bang. Craig cried out. Mum whirled round. Craig was slumped on the ground.

'Craig!' cried Dad, flinging himself down beside him. 'Craig!'

There was a rattle of stones. Two men carrying guns were coming out of the bush towards them.

⚮

Kal was stunned. The sound of the shot was still ringing in his ears. The men looked vaguely familiar: one was tall and the other shorter. He could just make out some words on the tall one's t-shirt.

Another scream from Mum, and Kal tore his eyes away. Craig was lying on the ground, and blood was spreading across his shirt. Dad was holding him, a look of horror on his face.

Craig didn't move.

Kal turned and ran. He had one thought: get help!

Another shot. It ricocheted off a rock. Another. A spurt of dust leapt up near his feet. He twisted and dodged between two trees. A bullet thudded into one them.

Kal whimpered, and tried to run faster.

Where's the plane? Where is it? He swerved round a rock and glanced over his shoulder. The taller man was after him. He had left his rifle, but in his hand was a *simi*, the sun glinting on the blade.

Where's the plane?

The man was gaining on him.

Kal swerved towards some bushes. Thorns tugged at him scratching his face, ripping his shirt, tearing his legs. He didn't slacken his speed. The man was behind him, floundering and cursing and hacking at the wait-a-bit thorn with his *simi*.

Kal had gained a few precious metres. He raced clear of the

bushes; his eyes were misting; he wiped his hand across them. Blood! He hardly noticed.

"*Jesus saves*". That was it! That was what was written on the man's t-shirt.

Kal darted round a clump of rocks, then another thicket of bushes.

He'd seen those men before – but where?

He looked back. No sign of the man.

The hotel! They were the guys he thought were going to nick the Range Rover!

Round another thicket. Still no sign of the man.

But what were they doing here?

Kal swerved to the left, ran a couple of hundred metres and threw himself down behind a jumble of rocks. 'Jesus saves. Please save me,' he whimpered.

His heart was pounding as though it would burst out of his chest, and a metal band was tightening round his heart. He was sucking in lungfuls of air, desperately trying to relieve the pain. Gradually, his breathing eased and the band loosened. He looked at his legs and arms – blood was streaming from numerous cuts and scratches. He felt nothing.

He raised his head.

Had he shaken off the man?

He listened.

There was no sound of pounding feet. No sound of panting breath. No chink of stones from someone creeping among the rocks. But there was a sound, a strange sound, a ridiculous sound – as though someone was sawing wood. The noise was coming from behind him.

He slowly turned his head.

There was a blur of movement. Kal twisted away just in time. The snake, its mouth wide open, was so close that its skin brushed his arm.

Kal's eyes were wide with terror. The snake was coiling and twisting, working itself into a frenzy. Kal was mesmerised. It wasn't a big snake, but it was thickset with a diamond pattern down its back. It drew its head back. Kal didn't wait. He hurled himself to the side and leapt up just as the snake struck again, missed, and thumped into the sand.

Kal ran.

He came clear of the rocks. And there ahead of him was the plane. But it was nearly a mile away!

His eyes caught a flash of sun on a *simi*. The man was walking slowly, studying the ground, following Kal's tracks. As soon as Kal appeared, he gave a shout and set off after him.

Kal could never outrun this man, a man who knew the bush, had lived all his life there. What hope did he have, even if he was a good runner – a twelve-year-old boy against a fully-grown man who hunted in the bush for his livelihood?

Kal looked back. The man was gaining on him.

Why hadn't he said something to Reuben when they were at the hotel? Why, oh why? Now it was too late.

Reuben!

Kal's mind suddenly cleared. His shoulders relaxed, his stride increased. He was no longer in the bush; he was in the Olympic stadium; the noise of the crowd was deafening; the hurdles and the water-jump flowed past; his chest was tightening; he shut out the pain; he forced his shoulders to relax; he had to keep his rhythm; he was coming off the final bend; he could see the line ahead; he threw his chest out; his arms began to pump; he dug into reserves he didn't know he had; he flew.

He tore open the door of the plane, and threw himself into the seat. The keys! The spare keys! Where does Craig keep the spare ignition keys? He scrabbled frantically in all possible hiding places. The sun visor. Yes! What do I do? He turned the ignition switch. Nothing. Think! Master switch. He tried again. There was a whirring sound. Think! Fuel primer.

'Come on, come on!' he yelled.

The engine sprang to life. No time to do the checks.

He opened the throttle. The plane juddered. Kal operated the foot pedals and turned onto the airstrip. The man was running towards him.

Kal set his mouth in a thin line, clenched his teeth, increased the revs, and raced towards the man.

The man threw his *simi*. It bounced harmlessly off a wing.

Kal held his line.

The man hurled himself aside just in time. The plane swept past, engulfing him in a cloud of dust.

Kal was away.

CHAPTER 13

Craig's plane

TERRIBLE NEWS

Lucy and Joel were carrying out some repairs to the orphan pens. Matata came and watched. At first, he was shy but when it came to feeding time, he joined in and helped. Lucy thought he might be rough with the animals, having been a poacher, but then she saw that he had a special way with them.

It was mid-afternoon before they finished, and Lucy was exhausted. 'Phew,' she said, 'that took ages.'

Joel smiled. 'Go and have some food, Lucy.'

She ran back to the house for a late lunch, and found her sister on the veranda reading a book.

'We've kept some lunch for you,' said Ellie, pointing to some dishes on the sideboard covered in a muslin cloth.

'Great,' said Lucy. 'I'm starving.' She drank two glasses of fresh limejuice, collected some food, and slumped down in a chair, with Fupi at her feet waiting for scraps. 'When do you think the others will be back?' she asked.

Ellie shrugged.

⋘⋙

Lucy had dozed off. She was woken by the sound of a vehicle. She hadn't heard the plane, but that would be Joel coming back with the others. She and Fupi ran out to meet them.

Then she stopped. Joel had only Kal with him.

Kal was getting out of the vehicle. His shirt was torn, he was covered in blood, and he was crying. He never did that – not even the time he broke his arm playing football.

'What is it?' she cried, rushing up to the vehicle. 'Kal, what happened to you? Where are the others?'

'Oh, Lucy!' cried Kal. 'Craig's dead.'

'What!' Ellie had come down the steps. 'What do you mean, dead?'

'Craig's dead – he's been shot.'

'No!' Ellie put her hands to her face. 'What about Mum and Dad?'

'They're okay, but, Ellie, he wasn't moving.'

'Dead!' wailed Lucy. And the three of them clung to each other. Fupi ran round them looking puzzled.

'I need to tell *Memsabu*,' said Joel, and hurried off.

A few moments later, Diana joined them. All the colour had drained from her face. 'Come inside, children,' she said, in a cracked voice. She led them to the veranda and made them sit down. Martha came in with mugs of tea and handed them round. She was crying.

Lucy put her tea on the side, threw her arms round Martha's neck and sobbed.

Then Diana said quietly: 'Joel has told me a bit, Kal. Can you tell us what happened?'

Lucy looked up but still clung to Martha.

Kal wiped his arm across his eyes and put his mug down. 'I think it was poachers,' he said. 'We were just about to have lunch when I saw these two men with guns. One of them pointed his gun at us and—' He put his head into his hands. '—there was this shot and Craig fell to the ground and... and there was blood coming from his chest and... Mum was screaming and Dad was holding him and—' He began to sob again. '—and I saw the men coming towards us, so I ran. I had to get help.'

'What happened?' asked Ellie.

'I ran to the plane and flew back.' He made it sound as though he'd ridden his bicycle back from school.

'You're covered in blood,' said Lucy.

'Lucy, Craig wasn't moving,' he whispered.

Samson came running. 'What happened?' he cried, rushing up to Kal's chair.

'I think they were poachers,' said Kal, and retold the story.

'You did well,' said Samson, gripping Kal's shoulder. 'Those men, did you recognise them?'

Kal nodded. 'The guys from the hotel. I thought they were going to nick the Range Rover.'

'What hotel? What Range Rover?'

Kal explained.

'So,' said Samson slowly, 'these men are working for Nagu. You're sure it was the same men?'

'Almost certain,' said Kal.

Samson stood up and took a mobile phone from his pocket. They all watched and waited as he dialled a number.

Samson tried again. 'It's no good; I can't get a signal. I'll try the radio.' He hurried into Craig's office.

More waiting. No one said anything; they just looked

anxiously at one another and tried to overhear what Samson was saying.

Finally Samson emerged. 'Either the police are not answering, or their radio's broken.'

'What can we do?' cried Lucy, panic rising in her voice. 'What will happen to Craig, and what about Mum and Dad?'

'We can't just leave them,' cried Ellie.

'I'll go out there with some of the men,' said Samson.

Diana shook her head. 'You can't go today, Samson. It will soon be dark; there's nothing you or anyone can do until it gets light.'

'No!' wailed Lucy.

Samson thought for a moment; then nodded. 'You're right, Diana. I'll tell Joel to fetch the cattlemen to spend the night here and we'll leave first thing in the morning.'

After supper, which no one felt like eating, they gathered round the table and discussed their plan. Lucy remembered that she and Kal had once watched a war film about some commandoes planning a raid; they had been sitting round a table the night before, just like this. But this was for real!

'Kal has to come to show us the way,' said Samson, 'but Lucy and Ellie must stay here.'

'No way!' cried Lucy. And she could see Ellie shaking her head.

'Samson's right,' said Diana, wiping her eyes, 'we cannot risk anyone else getting hurt.'

'But Mum and Dad are somewhere out there,' said Ellie, 'we can't stay here.'

'It's too dangerous,' said Samson.

'You can't stop us!' cried Lucy. 'We're coming with you.'

Diana shook her head. 'Samson and the others can't be responsible for you.'

'We can look after ourselves,' insisted Ellie. 'Lucy's right; we have to come.'

Diana sighed. 'What do you think, Samson?'

'I'm not happy.'

'Nor am I.'

'We're coming,' said Ellie quietly.

Lucy glanced at her sister. What a change from the Ellie who had arrived in Arusha and thrown a strop because her mobile wouldn't work.

Samson and Diana had a whispered conversation.

'All right,' said Samson, pursing his lips, 'but you stay with me at all times and do exactly as I tell you. Is that understood?'

The children nodded.

Samson stood up. 'I'll go and talk to the men.'

As soon as he had left, Diana turned to the children. 'You heard what Samson said – early start tomorrow. Off you go now.'

They murmured their goodnights and trooped off the veranda.

Lucy looked back at Diana, and saw silent tears starting. Poor Diana; Craig was her only son. Lucy rushed back and hugged her; then ran off to Ellie's *banda*, sobbing. There was no way she was going to be on her own tonight.

CHAPTER 14

Spring-hare

MATATA FINDS THE WAY

Lucy was alone in the forest. She was being followed. It was getting dark. She heard a horrible squeaky laugh. It was Moshi with the face of a toad! Lucy tried running faster, but couldn't see where she was going. She didn't know the way. She could hear heavy breathing. She tripped and tumbled into a great dark hole. Then, suddenly, there was Craig. He caught her and she clung to him. 'It's all right, Lucy; everything's all right.' He was smiling.

Suddenly she was wide-awake. 'Ellie, Ellie, wake up!' She sat up and shook her sister.

'What is it?'

'Ellie, wake up!'

'Leave me alone, I need to sleep.'

'But Ellie – everything's all right!'

Ellie sat up with a start. 'What do you mean?'

'It was Craig – he says that everything's all right.'

Ellie took Lucy in her arms. 'Lucy, it was a dream.'

Lucy slowly nodded. 'I suppose so, but it… it seemed so real.'

Ellie switched on a torch and looked at her watch. 'It's only just after two, Lucy; go back to sleep.'

'Ellie, don't you realise, we don't need to be sad – it's all going to be okay.' She could tell her sister was watching her in the dark. 'The dream was as real as you sitting here.'

'That's scary.'

'Ellie, it's true!'

◈

The next thing Lucy knew, Martha was shaking her. She and Ellie changed into their day things and hurried out to the veranda. It was still dark, but everyone was there. Martha and Matata were taking round mugs of tea. Three cattlemen, dressed in their Maasai warrior clothes, were sitting on the steps of the veranda, warming their hands on their mugs, but they weren't laughing and joking as they normally did, just chatting quietly. They wore *shukas* round their heads and shoulders against the cool of the night – it was only just after four – and Lucy could see, in the dim light from the veranda, their spears stuck in the ground beside them. She knew Onesmo; she particularly liked him, he was one of the men who had brought in Mondo. He had taken her several times to see the cows with calves, and had let her bottle-feed a calf whose mother had been killed by a lion. She recognised the other two, but couldn't remember their names.

Diana was talking to Samson and Joel, and Kal was sitting hunched up in a chair sipping his tea and gazing into the darkness.

Lucy longed to tell him that everything was going to be all right but she wasn't sure he'd understand.

'*Tuende* – let's go,' called Samson, putting his mug down and getting to his feet.

'Just a minute,' said Diana. She went into the office and returned with a rifle. 'You may need that.'

Samson held her eyes briefly, took the rifle, and nodded. 'I've got the radio; we'll keep in touch.'

Diana turned to the children. 'Come back safely.'

❧

Samson drove, with Matata and Kal beside him. Lucy and Ellie sat on the middle seat with Fupi between them. Joel and the three cattlemen sat behind. No one spoke.

It was the first time the children had been driving in the bush in the dark, and Lucy wished things weren't so tense, then they could have stopped and looked at the night animals that they glimpsed in the headlights: nightjars swooping to catch moths caught in the beam of the lights, a honey-badger bumbling off home, loads of spring-hares bouncing around like miniature kangaroos, and even a snuffly old aardvark. But today, game viewing was the last thing they were thinking about.

There was a crackle on the two-way radio and Diana's voice came through the darkness. 'How is it Samson? Over.'

'No problem. We expect to be at the place in about two hours. Over.'

'Good, let me speak to Kal. Over.' Samson passed the radio across.

'Kal, do you think you can find the place? Over.'

'Yes, I know where it is. Over.'

Lucy was sure that Kal had often imagined himself going off on an early morning raid – just like those commandoes in the film – and communicating in radio-speak with base, but he could never have imagined anything like this.

'Good luck. Keep in touch. Over and out.'

'Over and out.' Kal passed the radio back to Samson and continued to stare ahead.

It seemed almost no time before the sun came over the horizon. Samson turned off the headlights. The day quickly warmed up, and they took off their sweaters and threw them into the back.

The hills came gradually nearer, and Lucy began to worry. Had she really seen Craig? Was everything really going to be all right?

Samson and Kal were talking in low voices. Kal seemed to know exactly where to go. Lucy felt very proud of her brother – but she would never tell him that.

They arrived at the edge of the hills, and Kal pointed upwards. It was now very rough but the Land Rover kept moving forward like some willing workhorse ploughing through sand, scrabbling over rocks and flattening bushes in its relentless climb. They finally reached a plateau that Lucy recognised. 'This is where we built the airstrip,' she cried.

Kal nodded. 'See the tyre marks of the plane,' he said, pointing. 'We started from over there yesterday, by those trees.'

Samson drove across, and they climbed out and stretched their cramped limbs. Fupi started sniffing around, and Joel and Matata began searching for tracks.

'*Njia hapa*,' called Matata. The men gathered round him and peered at the ground.

'What is it, Ellie?' asked Lucy.

'Matata's found the way,' said Ellie.

Samson spoke briefly to Joel and Matata. They went to the back of the vehicle and returned almost immediately. Joel was carrying his spear, and Matata had his bow and arrows – he must have found where Craig had hidden them.

'Kal,' said Samson, 'can you describe the place where it all happened?'

Kal picked up a stick, and everyone squatted down on their haunches and watched him draw in the sand. There was much nodding and *eehing*. When Kal had finished, Joel and Matata stood up and shook everyone's hand then, without another word, crossed over a gully and went loping off, as effortlessly as gazelles, Matata's leg being now almost healed.

In five minutes they were out of sight.

'Good luck,' murmured Lucy.

'What do we do now, Samson?' asked Kal.

'We wait.'

Ellie went to the vehicle and came back with a tin of biscuits and some bananas. The cattlemen made a fire, and soon they were sitting in the shade nibbling the food and sipping tea.

'Should we call Diana?' asked Ellie.

'I'll do that,' said Kal, jumping to his feet. 'What shall I say?'

'Tell her we have arrived at the airstrip,' said Samson. 'Joel and Matata have gone to find the place, and the rest of us are waiting.'

Ellie ate another banana, and Lucy gave Fupi a biscuit.

Kal returned after a few minutes. 'Diana says, good luck.' He took a banana and sat down on his own, with his back to a tree, and gazed into space.

There was nothing to do but wait.

It seemed to Lucy that they had been there for hours, when Fupi pricked her ears and growled. The men, whom Lucy thought had gone to sleep, sat up instantly, their hands on their spears; but they relaxed when they saw a grinning Joel come loping into view, followed by Matata. Fupi ran over to them, sniffed them, wagged her tail, and being satisfied went and lay down in the shade of the vehicle.

'We found the place,' called Joel. 'And we found this.' He held up a small brass tube.

There were sharp intakes of breath from the cattlemen, and exclamations of '*aieeh*!'

'What is it?' said Lucy.

'Can I see?' said Kal.

Joel passed it to him.

'Probably a three-o-three,' said Kal in a flat voice.

'A what?' said Ellie.

'Cartridge from the bullet that killed Craig.' Kal was on the verge of tears again.

'But Craigi is not dead!' cried Joel. 'I think he is hurt but he can walk.'

'What!'

'*Kwele* – true. That one, he is strong like a buffalo – *kama nyati*.'

The cattlemen nodded in agreement and said '*eeh*'; then chattered away, huge grins on their faces.

'I knew it!' said Lucy. 'I said everything was going to be all right!'

Kal looked baffled.

'Did you see anyone?' asked Samson.

'No,' said Joel, 'but Matata found the way they went.'

'How many people?'

'Five.'

'That's Mum, Dad, Craig and the two men?' said Kal, his face now shining.

'We think,' said Joel. 'Those men, their tracks are the ones we saw the other day.'

He and Matata sat down on the ground and Ellie passed each of them a mug of tea.

'I'll radio Diana,' said Samson. When he returned, he gathered everyone together. 'Are we all ready – *tayari*?'

There were nods all round.

'Will you and Ellie be all right?' he asked, looking at Lucy.

She glanced at the men, hardened by life in the bush, and wondered if she and Ellie really would, but she was determined not to let it show. 'Yes,' she said.

Samson appeared doubtful, but all he said was: 'We have to move quickly and quietly.'

Lucy nodded.

Samson packed his rucksack with water and some food, collected the rifle, locked the Land Rover, and they set off across the gully, following Joel and Matata.

Lucy tried not to imagine too much, and not to think how hot it was, and how thirsty and weary she felt – *and* whether they might walk straight into an ambush and be shot!

They had been walking for an hour, when Joel stopped them and pointed to a patch of ground. 'This is where Craigi fell.'

Lucy peered; then blinked and rubbed her eyes. How on earth could Joel make sense of a few scuff-marks on the ground?

Matata indicated a dark bit on the sand. '*Damu.*'

'What's that, Ellie?' whispered Lucy.

'Blood.'

Although it was baking hot, Lucy couldn't help shivering. They had found a tiny patch of dark sand in the middle of Africa, and it was Craig's blood!

'*Hapa na hapa,*' said Matata, pointing at different places on the sand.

'He says, here and here,' whispered Ellie, 'but I can't see anything.'

'Nor can I,' whispered Lucy.

'See here,' said Joel, 'Craigi is now standing again.' The cattlemen peered and nodded. Lucy had given up trying to read anything into the marks on the ground, and just accepted what Joel was saying.

Joel, Matata and the cattlemen began scrutinising the ground and their surroundings, calling to each other and pointing out things. There was a shout from Onesmo, who was digging in a tree with his spear. A few minutes later he came over to Samson holding something in his hand. '*Risasi*,' he said.

'What is it, Samson?' asked Lucy.

'A bullet.'

'In the tree! How did it get there?'

Samson shrugged.

'Kal, do you know?' asked Lucy.

Kal had gone very pale. He took the bullet from Samson, and glanced at Lucy. 'No,' he said.

'*Hapa*,' called Matata.

'This is the way,' said Samson.

Kal slipped the bullet into his pocket.

'Is it much further?' asked Ellie, wiping her hand across her forehead. Her face was looking red.

'I don't know,' said Samson. 'Are you all right?'

'Yes,' said Ellie fiercely.

But Lucy could see she was struggling. *She* was, as well, but she knew they couldn't let these brilliant people down by being wimps.

'Have a drink,' said Samson.

'Thanks,' said Ellie. 'I'm fine. We should go on.'

Lucy couldn't understand how Joel and Matata could see where to go, but every now and then, one would point out something on the ground: a broken twig, a speck of blood, a disturbed rock, a crushed leaf; and the other would nod, and they would hurry on.

Eventually, they came to an open area where a small stream ran across bare rocks and disappeared over a ledge into a pool below. They stopped and splashed cool water over their faces and arms then crossed to the shade of a tree and ate the remaining bananas. Fupi went off to explore, and Kal took off his trainers and socks to paddle in the shallow stream. 'Come on, guys,' he called.

'Is it all right, Samson?' asked Ellie. She'd read about some nasty disease you could get by paddling.

'No problem, but be careful; it's very slippery.'

Ellie and Lucy joined Kal, and they splashed and slipped and slithered in the cool water, and for a moment forgot their worries and fears. Then they sat on the warm rocks letting the sun dry their legs. Lucy looked at the massive rocky hillside that rose up in front of them. Although she was feeling apprehensive about what lay ahead, she couldn't help gazing in awe at the scenery. What a beautiful country, she thought, and that rock face was truly magnificent. She could see what looked like caves higher up.

'I wonder if anything lives in those caves,' she said.

'Craig says leopards live in caves,' said Kal.

'And bats,' added Lucy.

'I don't like bats,' said Ellie, 'they get in your hair.'

'That's rubbish!'

'No, it's…'

'*Aieeh*!'

The children spun round.

Matata was yelling and pointing.

CHAPTER 15

Vultures soaring

THE PLACE OF THE SKULL

Everyone stared at Matata.

'*Mahali pa mfupa ya kichwa*,' he screeched, pointing at the rock face.

'What is it?' whispered Lucy.

'He says, it's the Place of the Skull,' said Ellie, in a strangled voice.

'Yes!' cried Kal. 'Look! Those caves we were looking at. There, see. Those could be two eyes, and the one below could be a mouth.'

'And that jagged bit in the middle could be the nose,' cried Lucy.

A cloud drifted across the sun, and suddenly it felt much cooler.

'I don't like this,' said Ellie.

Matata's eyes were wide with fear and he was trembling. Samson put a firm arm round his shoulders, but it took several minutes before he settled.

'It is the place, Samson, isn't it?' said Lucy.

He nodded. 'I think so.'

They looked at the rock face that earlier had seemed so majestic – now it appeared sinister and menacing. Vultures were soaring in the air currents rising above it.

There was a bark. Fupi was upstream, and they could see her sniffing at something on the ground, her tail wagging madly.

'Let's go and see.' Kal jumped up and ran across the rocks in his bare feet.

Lucy and Ellie followed.

'What is it, Fupi?' called Lucy.

Fupi looked up, her tongue was hanging out and she seemed to be grinning.

'What is... it's a hankie!' cried Lucy.

Kal picked it up: the initials SB were in one corner.

'It's *Mum's* hankie!'

They took it back to show the others.

'Well done!' cried Samson. 'Now, come and see what Joel found.' He led them across the rocks, and even Lucy could make out the remains of a fire.

Joel put his hand to it. 'It is still warm; I think they left about four hours ago.'

'So they spent the night here?' said Lucy.

'Yes, and they met someone.'

'How do you know?'

'There are now tracks of six people.'

Lucy shook her head in bewilderment. Life in Putney had never prepared her for anything like this.

'We must go on,' said Samson.

The children gathered up their socks and trainers, and as Lucy began to put hers on, she noticed a piece of greenish rock by her foot with a hint of red in it. But it wasn't brownish red like the other stones she'd found; this was a distinctive bluish red. And there was another piece. And another. She quickly slipped them into the pocket of her shorts without saying anything. She wasn't going to risk making a fool of herself again. She finished tying her laces, scrambled to her feet and hurried to catch up with the others.

After a while, the trail began to head downwards. They rounded the side of a hill and there was the plain below them, but the hillside was rough with thorny bushes and spiky trees that they had to skirt round. It would be some time before they reached the plain. They continued downwards. Every so often, Joel bent down to inspect the invisible trail or pick up a pinch of dust and let it float away to test the direction of the wind.

They were about half way down when Joel held up his hand. He turned his head and listened.

'What is it?' Lucy whispered.

'Shh.'

Samson unslung his rifle.

Lucy couldn't hear a thing – only birds.

Joel pointed with his *simi*. Samson lined up his rifle.

Lucy thought she heard a *tssk, tssk* sound. Some birds, about the size of starlings, flew up.

Joel put his finger to his lips and signalled them to move back.

Lucy looked nervously at him. 'What is…?'

'Go!' yelled Joel. He grabbed Lucy's arm and dragged her after him.

Onesmo had grabbed Ellie, almost carrying her.

Samson remained motionless, his rifle aimed straight ahead.

Kal and the others were already running.

There was a snort and crashing through the bushes just by where they had been standing.

Lucy glimpsed an enormous black shape that went careering down the hill.

Buffalo! They had nearly walked into a buffalo!

Joel stopped and let go of Lucy's arm. He was laughing.

'Joel!' cried Ellie. 'Someone could have been killed!'

He shrugged. '*Labda* – perhaps.' He was still laughing.

'And you can laugh!'

'No one *was* killed,' said Joel.

'Honestly!'

'How did you know the buffalo was there?' asked Lucy, still panting. 'I couldn't see a thing.'

'The birds,' said Joel.

'The birds – what birds?'

'Oxpeckers – tick birds,' said Samson, joining them and unloading the rifle. 'They feed on the buffaloes and act as watchmen.'

'*Macho ya nyati*,' said Matata.

'What's that mean?' said Lucy.

'The eyes of the buffalo,' said Samson. 'The birds have very good eyes and warn the buffaloes if anything is coming.'

'*Namna hii*,' said Matata, and gave the *tssk, tssk* sound that Lucy had heard.

'The wind changed,' said Joel, 'and he caught our smell.'

'Kal's feet, probably,' said Lucy.

'Hey, watch it!'

'Are we safe yet?' asked Ellie. The colour was beginning to return to her cheeks.

Joel nodded. 'He is now far. He was frightened.'

'*He* was frightened!' cried Ellie.

'It was a male on his own,' said Samson, 'those ones can be bad. Very bad.'

'I read that more people in Africa are killed by buffaloes than by any other animal,' said Lucy.

'*Kwele* – true,' said Joel.

'Great!' said Ellie. 'I find that really comforting.'

'At least, it's another bird for the list,' said Lucy.

'Poxy birds,' muttered Kal.

'You can say that,' said Lucy, 'but if it hadn't been for them we could have walked right into that buffalo.'

'Ner,' said Kal, 'I'd seen it; I was just about to warn you all.'

'Yeah, right,' said Lucy. 'We'll believe you.'

Samson handed round a water bottle; then they resumed their journey and reached the plain without further excitement. Lucy was relieved because she could now empty all the grit out of her trainers.

Joel pointed at the sand. 'Those ones have been picked by a vehicle.'

There was no mistaking the signs this time – even Lucy could see the tyre tracks.

'Is that the other man?' said Kal.

Joel nodded. 'Yes.'

There was a shout from Matata. They hurried over to where he was pointing at the ground.

'What is it, Matata?' asked Ellie.

Matata was indicating what looked like a game trail, going off in the opposite direction to the tyre tracks.

Ellie translated for Lucy. 'Matata says that two men have gone away on foot. He thinks they're the ones who captured Mum, Dad and Craig.'

Samson had a quick discussion with Joel and Onesmo; then the two of them ran off.

'Where are they going?' asked Lucy.

'To get the Land Rover,' said Samson. 'We will wait.' He led them over to some shade.

'Where did that other vehicle go, Samson?' asked Ellie. 'The one with Mum, Dad and Craig.'

'Joel thinks, there,' said Samson, pointing.

Matata hissed, and Lucy's fear welled up again. She could just make out a rundown *manyatta* in the distance.

CHAPTER 16

Spotted eagle-owl

ELLIE'S SCARY PLAN

It was almost dark by the time Joel and Onesmo returned with the Land Rover. There was a brief discussion, and Lucy could see Onesmo and the two cattlemen nodding and looking excited, but there was also a hard look in their eyes.

'What's happening?' Lucy whispered to Ellie.

'They're going hunting.'

'What for?'

'Don't be thick, Lucy,' said Kal.

'Those men!'

Samson nodded. He said a few words to the three men, who grasped their spears and ran off down the path. Lucy watched them go; their bounding gait reminded her of Joel and Matata, and of the Maasai she and Kal had seen on TV running in the London marathon.

The rest of them climbed into the Land Rover and they set off. It wasn't long before Samson had difficulty seeing the track, but it wouldn't be safe to turn on the vehicle's lights, so Joel and Matata got out and loped ahead to show the way.

The moon rose, bathing everywhere in ghostly light.

They had been driving for about twenty minutes, when Joel and Matata stopped. Joel came up to Samson's window. 'We are now close to that *manyatta*; Matata will go and see.'

'Shouldn't you go with him?' said Ellie.

'No,' said Joel, 'the dogs there know Matata; they won't worry if they smell him, but if I go they may give the alarm.'

Samson beckoned Matata over and whispered to him. Matata grinned and nodded. Samson looked worried as Matata disappeared into the darkness.

The rest of them climbed out of the vehicle and waited. This was the worst of all the waits that day. Lucy couldn't help worrying about Matata, about Onesmo and the two cattlemen, and she felt sick with worry about Mum, Dad and Craig.

A deep "*hoo hoo*" came from the darkness. Ellie whimpered, and although Lucy knew it was only an owl, she couldn't stop the hairs on the back of her neck rising. Another eerie hoot. Lucy wondered if it was an omen of terrible disaster to come. She peered at the tree from whence the sound was coming and thought she could just make out the silhouette of a massive eagle-owl in the bright moonlight. There was a hiss from the darkness. Fupi growled. Lucy nearly leapt out of her skin. Matata was back. He spoke urgently to Samson, who looked hugely relieved.

Ellie translated for Kal and Lucy. 'Mum, Dad and Craig *are* there,' she whispered.

Lucy gave a gasp of excitement.

'They have been put in a hut, and there are two men outside guarding with spears. Matata overheard them talking. It was someone the men called the Big Man who picked up Mum, Dad and Craig in the hills.'

'The Big Man – who's he?' whispered Lucy.

'Matata's not sure but he thinks it could be the one you call Toad Face,' said Samson.

'Toad Face!'

'Shh – yes, and he may come back tonight to get them.'

'What's Toad Face going to do?'

'Matata doesn't know.'

Samson started a whispered discussion with Joel. Samson seemed to suggest one thing, and Joel another, which Samson clearly disagreed with.

'What's happening, Ellie?' whispered Lucy, but Ellie was too intent on listening. Then she butted in. Samson and Joel seemed surprised to be interrupted by a girl, but they listened; then nodded; then they laughed and shook Ellie's hand. When she explained to Kal and Lucy, *they* didn't laugh. Ellie's plan was brilliant, but really scary.

They scrambled back into the Land Rover; Samson started the engine, turned the headlights full on, and set off.

There was no going back now.

The moon disappeared behind a bank of cloud.

Ellie had her eyes tightly shut. Why couldn't I keep my big mouth shut? What have I let myself in for? I could really screw up; then where will we be? And what'll happen to Mum, Dad and Craig?

Samson stopped the Land Rover.

Ellie opened her eyes.

The engine was still running and the headlights were

illuminating the *manyatta*. It looked even more sinister and rundown in the glare. Two men with spears were standing outside one of the huts, trying to shield their eyes.

'Go,' whispered Samson.

Ellie felt Lucy give her hand a squeeze. Her mouth was dry. She had forgotten her Swahili. It wouldn't work.

It *would* work.

It *had to* work.

Ellie slipped out of the vehicle and moved forward, being careful to keep behind the lights. She called out. The men with spears were staring straight at her. They didn't move. They must be able to see her. Her stomach knotted. She called out louder. The men whispered to each other. Ellie kept talking – now more insistent. One of the men went into a hut, and emerged with ole Tisip. Ellie's heart missed a beat. Ole Tisip looked furious and he was brandishing his club. She remembered it was called a *rungu*. What a time to remember that! Ole Tisip waved his hands at the blinding lights and shouted. Ellie kept talking. One of the men went inside the hut they had been guarding. Then, *Mum, Dad and Craig emerged*.

They stood blinking in the light, looking fearfully at ole Tisip waving his *rungu*. Ellie could see that Craig was holding his arm across his chest and his shirt was covered in blood. Her heart jolted, but she kept talking. The men with spears pushed Mum, Dad and Craig towards the light. Craig shouted something about turning out that confounded light, and Dad was complaining about something else. Mum seemed bewildered.

The three of them stumbled forward. As soon as they came clear of the lights, Kal, Joel and Matata grabbed them and bundled them into the Land Rover. Ellie shouted to ole Tisip, and ran to the back of the vehicle. Joel seized her, almost threw her in, and leapt in beside her. Samson shot backwards in reverse, slammed the vehicle into first gear and sped off, leaving the *manyatta* enveloped in dust.

Samson drove as fast as he dared along the sandy track, but it was a good minute before anyone spoke.

'Craig, what happened?' cried Lucy. 'Your shirt's covered in blood.'

'Probably looks worse than it is.'

'When... when you...' said Kal. 'I thought you'd been...'

'Mum's fainted!' cried Lucy.

'I can't stop,' said Samson, concentrating on the driving. He passed Lucy a water bottle. 'Use this.'

Lucy slopped water on Mum's face. 'Mum, Mum, are you okay?'

'Don't drown her!' cried Kal.

'*You* try sprinkling water while we're bumping along in the dark.'

Mum spluttered, shook her head and sat up. 'Where am I?'

Lucy handed her the bottle and she drank the remainder in one go. 'You're with us, Mum. You're all right.'

Mum shook her head and pushed her wet hair off her face. 'What happened?'

'We're the rescue party,' said Kal.

Mum burst into tears.

'Here.' Lucy put her arm round Mum's shoulder and gave her a hankie. 'You're safe now.'

'Thank you, darling.'

'We found your hankie, Mum.'

'This is mine? – the one I hid near the place where we spent the night!'

'Yes, we found where you dropped it – well, Fupi found it.'

'But what were... how did you...?' Mum shook her head again.

'Wasn't Ellie fantastic?' said Kal.

'Where *is* Ellie?'

'I'm here, Mum. Are you okay?'

Mum turned round. 'I'm so relieved to be away from that dreadful place. But how did you know we were there – and where's Mr Nagu?'

'Tell Mum,' said Lucy.

'I'm here, Mrs Bartlett,' came the squeaky voice from the back. 'I trust you enjoyed your stay at my friend's house.'

It was Ellie!

'I hope you were not inconvenienced, Mrs Bartlett.'

'Ellie! You were imitating him!'

'I was so scared,' said Ellie.

'Hey, man, that was incredible,' cried Craig, 'I was completely fooled.'

'So was I,' said Dad. 'But I must say I am very glad to be away from that place. Well done, all of you.'

'Have you changed your mind about Toad Face now, Dad?' asked Kal.

'Yes, I admit I misjudged him – not someone to trust.'

The children were all talking at once, telling Mum how Kal had raised the alarm, how they had called the men together, how they had travelled out in the vehicle, and how Joel and Matata had followed their tracks.

'And guess what?' cried Lucy. 'We've found the Place of the Skull.'

'What?' exclaimed Craig and Dad together.

'It's got to be the place,' said Kal, 'there's this rock face with caves and things in it that look like eyes and a mouth.'

'It's really spooky,' said Lucy.

'Where is it?' asked Craig.

'It's that place where we found Mum's hankie,' said Kal.

Lucy wondered. Should she tell them? 'Can I say something?'

'What, darling?' said Mum.

'I think I found some rubies there.'

'Not again,' muttered Kal.

Lucy ignored him. 'These ones look different; not like those barnetts we...'

'Garnets,' said Dad.

'Whatever. Can you look, Dad, when we get back.' She passed the stones to him.

Samson eased off the accelerator, letting the Land Rover find its way home. The moon emerged from behind the clouds, giving a magical radiance to the African night. They drove in contented silence. They would soon be back.

'I think there's a vehicle following us,' murmured Kal in a strained voice.

Samson muttered something and put his foot down on the accelerator.

The fear came flooding back.

CHAPTER 17

Buffalo

BUFFALOES

'Who is it?' asked Lucy, in a quavering voice.

'Nagu,' said Samson.

'Toad Face!'

'I don't like this,' said Craig. 'There's no knowing who he might have with him.'

'Go faster, Samson,' urged Ellie.

The vehicle sped along the rough track. Every time it hit a bump, Lucy heard Craig gasp with pain.

'He's getting closer,' said Kal.

They raced through some trees, the ghostly trunks flashing past and disappearing into the darkness. Almost immediately, the track branched three ways.

'Take the left,' shouted Craig, 'and turn your lights off. We may fool him.'

Samson switched off the lights. Despite the bright moonlight, it was hard to see and he had to slow down.

Lucy looked round. 'I think he's stopped,' she whispered. 'I think it's going to work. Yes! He's gone down one of the other tracks.'

'He's turning round,' yelled Kal.

'No!' cried Lucy.

'If that's Toad Face in his Range Rover,' said Kal, 'there's no way we can beat him.'

'It's still a good two miles before we get onto the ranch,' said Craig.

'What if he catches us?' cried Mum.

'Let's not find out,' said Craig. 'We'll try and lose him. Joel, you know this area, where can we go?'

Before Joel could reply, Samson swore and slammed on the brakes.

'What is it?' cried Lucy.

'There!'

Lucy gasped. Buffaloes! They had driven into the middle of a herd of buffaloes. Large dark shapes surrounded them, their eyes reflecting the moonlight.

Everyone in the vehicle held their breath.

Lucy heard the animals snorting. There was a jolt, as one brushed against the vehicle. Then another.

'We're probably all right as long as we don't alarm them,' murmured Craig.

'Don't alarm them, Samson,' whispered Ellie.

Samson edged forward, still with his lights off. One or two buffaloes tossed their heads, and Lucy saw their great horns. If any of them attacked the vehicle, the metalwork would offer little protection to those inside. Lucy shrank closer to Mum.

'Toad Face is right behind, now,' said Kal.

'He's trying to force his way through,' said Dad.

'Idiot,' muttered Craig.

Everyone in the Land Rover heard it: a bellow followed by a great crunch. One of the lights on the vehicle behind went out. Another crunch, and another. The other light went out.

'They're sorting him out big time!' yelled Kal.

'He'll be killed!' screamed Lucy.

'He is all right,' called Joel from the back of the Land Rover, 'those buffaloes are going.'

'So are we,' shouted Samson. He flicked on the lights and sped off.

Nothing was following now.

❧

It was almost midnight when they got back to the house. Diana and Martha hurried out to greet them. There were hugs all round and more tears, and as soon as Craig was settled on the sofa, all the different stories had to be retold.

Lucy peered at his wound while Diana dressed it. She'd never seen anyone wounded like that before, but she thought Diana might have done – all those lions and things she'd shot. She seemed to know exactly how to deal with it.

'We need to get you to hospital,' said Diana.

'Mother, don't fuss,' said Craig. 'I just need to rest.'

'Nonsense. It's a deep wound and could turn septic. You're going to Nairobi first thing tomorrow and that's that.'

'Nairobi!' exclaimed Lucy.

'Yes,' said Diana. 'I know it's in Kenya, but the local hospitals probably won't have the necessary facilities.'

'I can't fly with my arm like this,' said Craig.

'I'll fly you,' suggested Kal.

'You most certainly will not!' said Diana. 'Flying round the ranch is one thing – and what you did was marvellous – but flying to Nairobi is something quite different. Craig's licence would be cancelled immediately and he would never be issued with another.'

'We could say it was an emergency,' said Kal.

Diana smiled. 'I know you only want to help, Kal, but one escapade is quite enough – we are taking no more risks. Samson will drive him there first thing tomorrow.'

Lucy sat down beside Craig.

'You *are* going to be all right?' she whispered.

'Hey, man, what's this?'

'I'm sorry, Craig,' she sniffled, 'I just don't want anything to happen to you.'

'Here,' he dug into his pocket and pulled out his hankie.

'Thanks.' She wiped her tears and blew her nose. 'Sorry.'

Kal sat down on the other side of the sofa. 'You all right, Craig?'

'Wasn't Kal brilliant?' said Lucy.

'Not bad.' He winked at Kal. 'That was quite something – hey?'

'I'm not sure what was worse,' said Kal, 'being chased by that man, or nearly being bitten by that snake.'

'Snake?' said Lucy. 'You never told us about a snake.'

'I probably forgot.'

'You don't forget about something like that!'

'All right, but I had other things to think about.' Kal described the incident.

Craig slowly shook his head. 'You are so lucky – that joker is about the worst we have.'

Kal turned pale. 'What was it?'

'Saw-scaled viper: one of the deadliest snakes in Africa – in the world. Gets its name from the noise it makes rubbing its scales together when it's angry.'

'Huh.' Kal fingered the bullet in his pocket. Better not tell them about that, he thought.

'Well, well,' came a voice from the far end of the veranda. Dad was beaming, the light from the microscope reflecting on his face.

'What?' called Lucy.

'Lucy, I think you are right this time.'

'How do you mean?'

'I need to get confirmation, but I think the stones you collected from that place, the...'

'Place of the Skull?'

'Indeed. They appear to me to contain some excellent samples of ruby.'

Lucy didn't remember much after that, except everyone talking at once.

CHAPTER 18

Kori bustard

KIBOKO RIVER

Lucy woke next morning to the sound of voices. She sat up and looked out of the window. It was just getting light. Three men were sitting on the veranda steps, their *shukas* round their shoulders, and their spears stuck into the ground nearby. It was Onesmo and the other cattlemen; they'd walked all the way through the bush in the dark! She dressed and hurried outside.

'*Jambo*,' she called. 'What happened?'

'*Jambo, jambo sana*,' they replied, grinning.

'Was everything all right – *nzuri*?'

'*Nzuri, nzuri,*' they chorused.

She and the men grinned at each other. 'So it really was *nzuri?*'

'*Nzuri, nzuri,*' they repeated.

They tried telling her something, but she couldn't understand what they were saying. Then Lucy remembered another word.

'Would you like some *chai* – tea, *chai?*'

'*Ndiyo, ndiyo,*' they nodded. '*Nzuri, nzuri.*' By saying every word twice, they probably thought it would help her to understand.

She hurried through to the kitchen. Martha was setting out mugs, and the kettle was nearly boiling.

'*Jambo*, Martha.'

'*Jambo*, Lucy, *habari ya asubuhi?*'

'What does that mean?'

'How are you this morning?'

'*Nzuri, nzuri.*'

Martha clapped her hands.

Ellie came in. 'Those three men are back,' she said.

'I know, I was talking to them,' said Lucy, 'at least trying to.'

She and Ellie carried the tea out. The men made room on the veranda steps, and Ellie began chatting to them. There seemed to be a lot more *nzuri-ing* and some *eehing*, and plenty of nodding. Fupi came and joined Lucy.

'Ellie, what are they saying?'

'I'm finding out how they are.'

'Is that all?'

'It's very rude to ask direct questions.'

'Did they find the men? '

'Lucy!'

'Sorry.'

Finally, Ellie turned to Lucy. 'Lucy, they *did* find the men;

they had lit themselves a fire and the smell of the smoke gave them away. Onesmo and the other two waited until they were asleep; then crept up, removed their guns and fired them off.'

'Brilliant!'

'They say the men were so frightened that they won't stop running until they get to Kenya.'

Lucy looked at the men who were nodding and laughing at what Ellie was saying; they didn't look at all frightening now, but she remembered the look of determination in their eyes when they had set off.

Onesmo lay on the ground pretending to be one of those men. The others made banging noises, and Onesmo jumped up, leapt around, then started running in circles and shouting. Fupi barked. The other two men were holding their sides with laughter.

'What's all this *kelele* about?' Craig had appeared; he was looking tired but much better than last night. Lucy noticed blood had seeped through his bandage.

'How are you?' she asked.

'Better now, thanks to a good night's sleep.'

Ellie fetched him a mug of tea. He said something to the men then joined them on the steps. The men looked serious for a moment then one of them gave a repeat performance, with Craig joining in the laughter.

Kal arrived looking bleary-eyed. 'Aren't these the guys who went after those men?'

Craig explained.

'Do you think they'll come back?'

'No ways – they're probably thinking they're lucky to be alive.'

'What about the guns?' asked Kal.

Onesmo got up and disappeared round the side of the building, returning a few moments later carrying three guns.

'My rifle!' exclaimed Craig. 'I didn't expect to see that again.' He carefully checked it over.

'What will happen to the other guns?' asked Lucy.

'I'll hand them over to the police.'

The sun was now well up, and Martha was busy setting the breakfast table. Ellie went to help her. After shaking hands with everyone, the three cattlemen left. Kal and Lucy stayed sitting either side of Craig as they watched the sun rise and light up the ranch.

✎✎✎

Samson brought his Land Rover round to the veranda as soon as they'd finished breakfast, and Lucy was surprised to see that Dad was also ready to leave.

'Must strike while the iron's hot,' he said. 'I'd like to get confirmation on those samples, and Craig has kindly agreed that I travel with him to Nairobi. I'm pretty sure I'm right, but my knowledge in some areas is less than...'

'It looks as though everyone's ready,' said Mum, smiling brightly.

'Ah, yes, right oh. Goodbye, then.' Dad picked up his bag and went down the veranda steps to the vehicle. 'See you soon,' he called, as he climbed in. He put his head out of the window. 'This is really most exciting; I hope I can come back with good news.'

'Bye, Dad,' chorused the children.

They all trooped down to the vehicle. Kal carried Craig's bag and loaded it into the back; then they all stood around wondering what to say.

'Come back soon,' said Lucy.

He smiled. 'Take care, Lucy.'

She nodded – and sniffed a bit.

Everyone said goodbye, and Craig climbed in.

The children watched and waved until they could no longer see the vehicle's dust cloud; then Ellie fetched a book, Kal and

134

Matata went to play football, and Lucy collected her diary and a blanket, lay down in the shade of a tree with Fupi – and went to sleep.

Diana had a message on the radio from Samson early next morning, to say that Craig had been treated at the hospital for a chipped collarbone and a deep flesh wound from which a bullet had been removed.

'He is extremely lucky,' said Diana, 'it could have been so much worse.'

Lucy shuddered and tried not to think about it. 'When will he be back?' she asked.

'I don't know, dear, the hospital want to keep him under observation for the next few days,' said Diana, 'but one thing is certain, Craig will want to get back as soon as possible. He hates being in Nairobi.'

'Any news from Dad?' asked Ellie.

'Only that Samson is taking him to the geology department in the university today to meet a Professor Wafula.'

'He'll enjoy that,' said Kal. 'Dad likes meeting important people.'

'Mum, do you think Dad was right about those stones?' asked Lucy, 'about them containing rubies and sapphires and things?'

'I do hope so. You know how careful he is about his work.'

'But he could be wrong?'

'Lucy, there is no sense in speculating about what might or might not be, let's wait until he gets back.'

Lucy glanced at Ellie and Kal. She could tell they were also worrying about what might happen to Simba Ranch if Dad was wrong and Craig couldn't get extra money to run it.

Three days later, Diana announced that Craig, Dad and Samson would be leaving Nairobi the next day.

'It's at least an eight-hour drive,' she said. 'They won't be here before mid-afternoon at the earliest. Why don't you children go with Joel and Matata, take a picnic and meet them at the Kiboko River. It's a lovely spot; Joel knows it.'

It was just the three children, Matata and Fupi, who travelled there with Joel next day. When they arrived they climbed out of the Land Rover and surveyed a wide expanse of dry sand.

'But this isn't a river,' said Lucy, 'where's all the water?'

'Come, I will show you,' said Joel.

Kal parked the Land Rover in the shade of a large thorn tree. A pair of brown parrots – another for Lucy's bird list – flew out with screeching cries of annoyance at being disturbed.

They set off, Joel carrying his spear, Matata a *simi*, and Lucy her binoculars and bird book. The glare off the pale sand made them screw up their eyes as they followed the broad expanse of the sand river upstream. Vervet monkeys peered at them from the trees along the edge, making alarm calls at Fupi who was trotting beside Lucy; grey and white go-away birds mocked them with their *gowarrr* calls; iridescent bee-eaters swooped to catch dragonflies; and doves called from all around.

Lucy was becoming used to the wealth of wildlife everywhere but she still found it bewildering. She was trying to stay with the others but had to keep stopping to check out yet another new bird.

'Come on, Lucy,' called Kal.

'Coming. I've just seen a three-banded courser.'

'Three-banded corset! I bet Mrs Sandford wears one of them.'

'No, you wally, a courser.'

'Whatever, but don't take all day.'

They came round a bend in the sand river. There was still no sign of water, but an enormous greyish brown bird, almost twice the size of the ground hornbills Lucy had previously seen, was poking about in some grass. It looked up as they appeared, and then stalked off. Lucy was frantically juggling binoculars and book, before finally identifying it.

'It's a kori bustard,' she cried.

'Great,' said Kal, 'I've always wanted to see one.'

'It's Africa's heaviest flying bird,' said Lucy, reading from her book.

'It wasn't flying,' said Kal.

'Oh, for goodness…!'

Matata hissed and sniffed the air. He put his finger to his lips and hurried them out of the sand river.

'What is it?' whispered Lucy, when they had scrambled up the steep bank.

Matata said nothing, but beckoned and led them through the trees, continually looking around, testing the wind, and checking the ground. He led them past a clump of bushes; a pair of doves flew up with a clatter of wings, and a ground squirrel scampered off. He pointed.

Lucy gasped and snatched up Fupi.

There in the sand river stood an enormous elephant – no more than thirty paces away.

'It's not Moshi?' she whispered anxiously.

'No,' whispered Joel. 'This one is a male. He is peaceful.'

And there, at last, was the water. The elephant had dug a hole in the sand with his tusks; it must have been more than a metre deep. He was dipping his trunk into the water at the bottom, sucking it up and squirting it into his mouth. Some impala were standing nearby waiting for their turn, but from the leisurely way the elephant was drinking, it would be quite a wait.

As they watched, some zebras and baboons came and joined the queue. But a young male baboon, which was feeling thirsty or impatient, scampered to the water's edge and began to drink. The elephant sucked up a trunk full of water, gave a deafening scream and squirted the baboon, which fled with terrified shrieks.

The children couldn't stop themselves from laughing. The elephant looked in their direction. They froze. The elephant seemed to frown, then flapped its great ears, and resumed its drink.

Lucy breathed out.

Joel signalled them to move back. 'That is where the water is, Lucy,' he said, 'under the sand. It is only a proper river in the rains – then it can be very dangerous to try and cross.'

'How did Matata know the elephant was there?' asked Kal.

Joel pointed to the ground. Footprints, like enormous dinner plates, led towards the river. 'You can see by the big footsteps that it is a male elephant.'

'You and Matata may be able to, but I can't,' said Lucy.

'And see, here,' said Joel, pointing with his spear at scuff-marks in the sand between the dinner plates. 'That is where his nose marks the sand.'

'His trunk,' said Lucy. 'Those marks are made by his trunk?'

Joel nodded. 'Can you smell that?' he said, lifting his face and sniffing.

Lucy sniffed. 'It's a sort of farmyard smell.'

'That's the elephant,' said Joel. 'The wind is blowing towards us, so we can smell him, but he can't smell us.'

'What would happen if the wind was blowing the other way?' asked Kal.

'That one would get angry.'

'And what would he...' Lucy's words were cut short.

'*Ona!*' Matata was pointing to a distant hillside.

'What is it, Matata,' asked Ellie. 'What can you see?'

'I can't see anything,' said Lucy.

'It is Samson, returning,' said Joel. 'Look with your binoculars, Lucy.'

She put them to her eyes and searched the hillside. Eventually she located a minute dust plume moving down the hill. And Matata had seen that!

'Come,' said Joel. 'We will meet them.' He led them back to the Land Rover. They sat in the shade and ate their picnic, and watched some baboons foraging under the trees on the opposite bank. Lucy added a striped kingfisher to her bird list.

'What are those tracks that Fupi's sniffing?' asked Ellie, pointing to a trail that led across the dry sand towards the baboons.

Matata went and examined it. '*Simba*,' he called, '*dume*.'

Joel joined him; then beckoned the children down. Lucy was glad the Land Rover was nearby.

'It is a big male lion,' said Joel. 'See those feet. He has gone that way.' He pointed in the direction of the baboons on the far bank.

'Is he near?' asked Ellie.

'No, he crossed last night. He is now far. See, the baboons are not worried.'

Kal put his hand down and spread his fingers over one of the paw marks but couldn't cover it. 'I wouldn't want to mess with him,' he said.

'Someone's coming,' whispered Lucy, 'look.'

They stared. A man was pounding along the track towards them.

CHAPTER 19

Angry lion

AN ANGRY LION

The man saw them, waved and ran to join them.

'It's Reuben!' cried Kal.

'*Jambo*,' said Reuben, coming and shaking everyone's hand.

'Reuben,' said Lucy, 'what are you doing here?'

'Taking exercise.'

'Yes, but…'

'Look there's Samson,' said Kal, as a Land Rover came into view.

'And there's Craig,' cried Lucy, 'and Dad.'

Samson pulled up, and he, Craig and Dad climbed out of

the Land Rover and stretched their arms and shoulders.

The children hurried across. Lucy hugged Dad, then rushed up to Craig, who had his arm in a sling. 'Welcome back,' she cried.

'Thanks, Lucy.' He was smiling, and Lucy could see that the tired look had left his eyes. Pain could make people look tired, she thought. Craig had been so brave.

'How many bullets did they pull out?' asked Kal, grinning.

'About six,' said Craig, 'I lost count.'

Ellie's eyes widened. 'You are going to be all right, aren't you?'

'Yeah, but the doc says I'll never play the violin again.'

'I didn't know you played the...'

'Ellie – it's a joke,' said Lucy.

Ellie blushed. 'Sorry.'

'You'll still be able to fly?' said Kal.

'No sweat. So how are you guys?'

'We've just seen the most enormous elephant,' said Lucy, 'we were so close and...'

'Tell me as we drive back, Lucy,' said Craig. 'I'll swap places with Joel.'

'Can I drive?' asked Kal.

'Sure.'

☙❧

What Kal found was so fantastic about the dirt roads on the ranch was there were no pedestrians, no other traffic, no speed limits, and no parking restrictions. Their surface reminded him of the running track where he trained every Tuesday night; they were a similar colour and had a...

There was a loud bang.

Lucy screamed.

Kal's immediate thought was a shot. The steering wheel was snatched from his hands. He hit the brakes. The Land Rover veered off the track and stopped against a tree. 'What was that?' he cried, looking round wildly.

'Blow-out,' said Craig.

'What happened?' cried Lucy, rubbing her forehead where it had banged on the windscreen.

'We've got a burst tyre,' said Craig. 'Now you know, Kal, why I make you keep your thumbs outside the steering wheel on these roads.'

Kal looked at his hands. 'I guess that would have broken them.'

'Big time,' said Craig, climbing out of the vehicle.

Kal glanced at Lucy and made a face; then they both got out. Samson pulled up in the other Land Rover, and he and Joel came to inspect the damage.

'Have you got a spare?' asked Lucy.

Craig nodded. 'It'll take about ten minutes to change.'

Joel pulled out the high-lift jack from under the rear seat, and Samson found the wheel-brace and began loosening the wheel-nuts.

'Can I help?' asked Reuben.

'No, we are fine,' said Samson.

'Perhaps I'll carry on running, then. I need the training.'

'Rather you than me,' said Craig, grinning.

'Come on, Kal,' said Reuben, 'you can show me the way.'

'Me!' cried Kal, in alarm.

'Why not? You're wearing shorts and trainers.'

'Yes, but…'

'*Tuende* – let's go then.'

'Crumbs,' said Kal.

Matata took off his flip-flops.

'Are you going to run as well?' exclaimed Lucy. 'In bare feet!'

Matata grinned.

'I hope you two won't leave me behind,' said Reuben.

Kal turned and waved, and nearly tripped over a rock.

'We'll catch you up,' called Craig.

Kal couldn't believe it: he already had Reuben's autograph – but this! He was actually running with Reuben Kalima, with one of Tanzania's great athletes – one of the world's great athletes – a man who had won an Olympic gold medal.

He kept glancing at Reuben, noticing the way he held his arms, how he kept his shoulders relaxed, and how his flowing stride was effortless. He tried to relax in the same way and to copy that stride. His running became easier, *and* he was going faster. This was it! This was how he'd got away from that man in the hills.

Reuben smiled and nodded.

Kal grinned back. This was awesome. His own running now seemed effortless. The three of them were eating up the ground.

The track led them through clumps of bushes. They came round one of these and Kal, who was leading, skidded to a halt. Reuben and Matata nearly bumped into him.

A massive lion, its front paws on the body of a freshly killed zebra, was in the middle of the track. It looked up, startled.

It was a fully-grown male and its muzzle was covered in blood.

Kal was transfixed. His mouth dropped open in terror.

The lion stared unblinkingly at them and swished its tail slowly back and forth.

Kal felt his heart pounding. He tried to control his breathing, but it still sounded like a steam train. He hoped the lion couldn't hear it. His one urge was to run – but he knew that would be fatal.

'*Enda nyuma* – go back,' whispered Reuben. '*Pole pole* – slowly.'

Kal didn't dare look behind. He was mesmerised by the lion's cold yellow eyes. His head was beginning to swim.

The three of them edged slowly backwards, watching those unblinking eyes.

The lion climbed over the carcase and crouched down, still staring at them. Where was Craig? Why weren't the Land Rovers coming?

The lashing of the tail increased, and the lion started to creep towards them, never taking its eyes off their faces. The muscles in its shoulders rippled and its great paws padded noiselessly on the ground. They *were* bigger than Kal's hand – much bigger!

Reuben gave a quiet hiss and they stopped.

The lion stopped. It crouched lower and laid its ears back; then it started forward again. It made no sound: no growling, no roaring, no snarling. It just came slowly and silently towards them. Any moment, it would spring, and that would be it.

Kal found he was completely detached from what was happening, and wondered whether he would feel much. He'd seen, on TV, the way lions killed zebra and wildebeest. Did they kill people in the same way?

He was vaguely aware of a blur of movement.

The lion yelped as a rock hit its nose. Matata picked up another rock, ran at the lion with a great shout, and threw it.

This was too much. The lion turned and fled with Matata in pursuit.

Reuben and Kal yelled, and Matata stopped. He hurled another rock. Another yelp, and the lion disappeared into some bushes.

Matata came loping back, a huge grin on his face.

'Matata, that was awesome,' said Kal reverently.

They looked round at the sound of a vehicle. Craig drew up beside them. 'How's it going, guys?'

'I think I've done enough running,' said Kal.

They were now back at the house. Dad had gone off for a shower, Mum and Diana had finished fussing over Craig and disappeared inside, and Craig and Reuben were in Craig's office discussing ranch business, leaving the girls on the veranda listening to Kal's account of Matata's heroics.

'That guy was just so cool,' said Kal. 'I don't know what would have happened if...'

Fupi pricked up her ears and gave a soft growl.

They all looked up. Two vehicles were approaching the house. One was a police car and the other was a Range Rover with broken headlights.

CHAPTER 20

Club or rungu

REUBEN TURNS THE TABLES

Lucy watched fearfully as the vehicles drew up. 'Craig,' she called, 'I think you should come.'

'What is it?'

'Looks like trouble, big time,' said Kal.

Craig emerged from the office. Reuben stayed inside. 'What the…!'

Two policemen got out of the car, and Toad Face and ole Tisip got out of the Range Rover. They looked up briefly; then Toad Face led the way onto the veranda.

'Good afternoon, Gideon,' said Craig, looking hard and cold.

Toad Face ignored Craig's greeting but urged on one of the policemen. He looked very unhappy as he came forward.

'Mr Craigi, I have a warrant for your arrest,' he said, holding up a piece of paper.

'Arrest! What for?' cried Craig. He didn't move.

'For abduction.'

'Abduction!'

The policeman looked at the paper. 'Abduction of a boy, Lengurai ole Punyua.'

'Does he mean Matata?' whispered Lucy to Ellie.

Ellie nodded.

'No!'

'What is all this, Gideon?' said Craig.

'You heard what the officer said,' replied Toad Face, in his silly voice. He urged the policeman forward, who looked even more unhappy.

'Mr Craigi, I must ask you to come with us for further questioning in connection with this matter.'

'And, it would also be an opportunity,' added Toad Face, 'for you to tell the police why you have illegally taken over the land, known as the Seki Hills, that belongs to my friend ole Tisip.'

'Gideon, that's Simba land and you know it!' snapped Craig.

'I think you will find that the land registry document says something else.'

Craig said something rude.

Toad Face ignored it. 'The boy will be coming back with us to his proper home.'

'No, he won't!' cried Kal.

'Yes, he will, my small friend.'

'And if we refuse?' said Craig.

'It is called obstructing the police in the course of their duty. The courts do not view such behaviour sympathetically.'

Craig's lips were tight. 'Kal,' he said, 'go and get Matata.'

'No!'

'Kal, just go – trust me.'

Kal looked fearfully round and ran off.

Reuben was still in the office. Lucy didn't know whether or

not he could hear what was going on, but she wished he'd come out. She didn't dare move to go and get him.

Mum and Diana appeared from inside the house, and looked in alarm when they saw the new arrivals and everyone looking worried.

'Lucy, what is it?' whispered Mum.

'Toad Face and that other man want to take Matata away. They said something about Craig had abducted him. And they want to arrest Craig.'

'No!'

'Ah, Mrs Bartlett, good afternoon,' said Toad Face. 'I trust you have recovered from your little ordeal the other day.'

Mum glared at him. He looked very sure of himself. Ole Tisip looked venomous and was tapping his *rungu* against his leg. And the policemen looked extremely unhappy, but Lucy was relieved to see they made no move to put Craig in handcuffs, or whatever it was they did in Tanzania when they arrested people.

Kal and Matata returned. When Matata saw what was happening, he made to run off but one of the policemen grabbed his arm.

'Let him go!' yelled Ellie.

'Enough of this nonsense,' snapped Toad Face. 'We are taking this boy back to his home, and you, Craig, are under arrest for abduction and for further questioning.' He turned to the two policemen. '*Tuende* – let's go.'

'Just a moment, Mr Nagu.' Reuben emerged from the office.

The two policemen saw who it was, sprang to attention and saluted.

Reuben nodded briefly to them.

Lucy almost shouted for joy.

'Inspector Kalima – what are you doing here?' Toad Face had a startled look on his face.

'Just visiting,' said Reuben. He held out his hand to the

policemen who was holding the arrest warrant. The man passed it over. Reuben looked briefly at it, tore it up, and dropped the pieces on the floor.

'How dare you!' cried Toad Face.

'You must excuse me, Mr Nagu' continued Reuben, 'but I couldn't help overhearing what you were saying.'

Toad Face looked livid. 'So?'

'I understand you are about to leave,' said Reuben. 'Before you do, there are a few points that perhaps need clearing up.'

'Such as?'

Reuben took out some papers from a folder tucked under his arm. 'James Msolla, Simba's solicitor, has just had these drawn up. He asked me to bring them here,' he said, offering the papers across.

Toad Face made no effort to take them.

Reuben sighed. 'Let me explain then: these are court papers relating to one Lengurai ole Punyua, known by the name of Matata. If you were to read them, you would see that the boy is now the legal ward of Samson and Martha Mutugi of Simba ranch in the district of Shinyanga. Adoption procedures will shortly be finalised.'

'Hurray!' cried Lucy. She wasn't sure what it all meant, except that Matata was safe.

Now it was Toad Face's turn to look stunned, but the policemen were hugely relieved, and the one who was holding Matata's arm let go. Matata seemed bewildered, but Ellie hurried over to him and explained.

'Do you have anything you wish to say, Mr Nagu?' asked Reuben.

'This man and I are leaving.' Toad Face turned and indicated that ole Tisip should follow him.

Reuben nodded to the policemen and they barred the way.

'What is this?' raged Toad Face.

'As I said, Mr Nagu, there are a few points that need clearing up,' repeated Reuben.

'Stop wasting my time, Kalima!'

'A moment, please,' said Reuben. 'I believe Craig has something he would like to ask you.'

'What?'

'A number of things,' said Craig. His eyes were hard. 'Firstly: why did one of your men try to kill me?'

'Those were not my men.'

'They were!' cried Kal. 'I saw them in your Range…'

'They were employed by ole Tisip to protect his property.' Toad Face glared at Kal. 'I understand the one who shot you, Craig, was acting in self-defence.'

'That's monstrous!' cried Mum. 'Craig wasn't even holding his rifle when your man shot him.'

Toad Face shrugged. 'I wasn't there; it's your word against his.'

'How dare you!'

Toad Face ignored Mum's outrage and tried to barge past the policemen, but they blocked the way.

'Let me pass!'

'Mr Nagu,' said Reuben quietly, 'I believe you mentioned the Seki Hills.'

Toad Face spun round and glared at him. 'They belong to ole Tisip.'

'I don't think that is correct.'

'If you don't believe me, go and look at the land registry document.'

'I have,' said Reuben, 'and it shows that the land known as the Seki Hills on the Simba ranch is indeed registered in the name of Temes ole Tisip and, I might add, Gideon Nagu.'

Toad Face sneered at Craig. 'So, no more trespassing! And next time, my guards may not be quite so kind to you.'

Reuben raised his eyebrows, took a notebook out of his pocket and scribbled something. 'I thought you said the guards worked for ole Tisip,' he observed.

'Don't try and be clever, Kalima.'

'Very well,' said Reuben, 'perhaps then, we could return to discussing the Seki Hills. The document to which you refer is a forgery.'

'Rubbish!'

Lucy noticed flecks of white spit forming in the corners of Toad Face's mouth, and his eyes looked all piggy as he tried to contain his rage. 'This is disgraceful!' he snarled. 'You produce a totally false accusation without a shred of evidence.'

'I have the evidence,' said Reuben, looking quietly confident. Lucy could just imagine him lining up for the start of the Olympic final – he probably had that same look then.

'I don't believe you.' Toad Face tried to remain self-assured but uncertainty was creeping into his voice.

'Let me remind you, Mr Nagu, of a bit of local history,' said Reuben, going to the sideboard and pouring himself a glass of water. 'As you know, I was posted for a while to the nearby police station at Shinyanga, and certain things happened during my time there that we could not explain.'

'I'm not interested.'

'Just hear me. One thing was the disappearance and probable murder of a respected Maasai elder: Punyua ole Matunya, that boy's father.' He pointed to Matata, whose eyes were darting wildly between Reuben and Toad Face as he tried to follow what was being said.

'What are you accusing me of?'

'Nothing,' said Reuben mildly, 'I am merely telling you about some of the things that puzzled us. Another was, who was behind the persistent attempts to claim parts of Simba land?' He paused. 'Some of those questions are now beginning to make sense.'

'This is pure speculation, Kalima, and you know it.'

Reuben sighed. 'I will need to revisit the papers relating to the death of Matata's father…'

Toad Face snorted.

'… and I may want to question certain people in the light of remarks I have heard today.'

Toad Face glared. 'I warn you, Kalima, I have powerful friends and greatly resent your outrageous speculation.'

Reuben took a sip of water, but his eyes never left Toad Face. 'Mr Nagu, as far as the ownership of the Seki Hills is concerned, there *is* very little speculation.'

'Precisely,' snapped Toad Face, 'they belong to ole Tisip.'

'I don't think so,' said Reuben. 'You see, when Craig informed James Msolla and me, about a year ago, of a dispute relating to the Hills, the three of us went to the archivist in the Ministry of Land and Housing – who, incidentally, is a friend of Msolla's.'

'What's an archivist?' whispered Lucy to Ellie.

'Someone who looks after documents,' Ellie whispered back.

'Oh.'

'We explained the situation to him,' continued Reuben, 'and he showed us the land registration document. There was no doubt, at that time, that the Seki Hills were included in the land belonging to Simba Holdings, the company in whose name the ranch is legally registered.'

Toad Face started to say something, but Reuben held up his hand. 'A few months after our meeting, I received a call from the archivist telling me that someone else had asked to consult the same document. In view of our concerns, he thought I might be interested to know. That person, Mr Nagu, was you.'

'So? Those are public documents; I have every right, as MP for the area, to consult them.'

'Of course. But now, Mr Nagu, we get to the interesting part. A few weeks ago, the archivist informed me that you returned *again* to consult the document. Imagine his surprise when he discovered that the original document had been removed and replaced with a forgery (and not a very good one), showing the Seki Hills registered in your name and that of ole Tisip.'

'Don't you accuse me of forgery,' snarled Toad Face. His eyes narrowed. 'I'm warning you.'

Reuben paused. 'Mr Nagu, perhaps I did not make myself clear. I apologise; what I just said is not quite true.'

'Hah!'

'What I should have said, was that the archivist found that the *copy* of the original document had been removed. He is a cautious man, and following your initial interest, he replaced the original document (the one that shows Simba Holdings as the rightful owners of the Seki Hills) with a copy. It was the copy that was removed; the archivist still holds the original.'

Toad Face looked like a deflated football. 'It's not true,' he whispered. But Lucy could tell he knew he was beaten.

Reuben nodded at the policemen. 'Take them away.'

'Your vehicle looks a bit the worse for wear,' called Craig, as Toad Face and ole Tisip were led down the steps. 'Did you have an accident or something?'

Toad Face's eyes narrowed. 'You haven't heard the last of this,' he snarled.

Craig smiled. 'I think we have.'

There were sighs of relief all round as the men left.

'Thank goodness you were here to sort that out for us, Reuben,' said Diana.

'I was really worried,' said Lucy.

'What will happen to...' Ellie's words were cut short by a crash and a shout that was followed almost immediately by a revving engine. The next thing they saw was Toad Face's Range Rover being driven off at high speed.

CHAPTER 21

Angry elephant

MOSHI

They rushed to the edge of the veranda. The windscreen of the police car had been smashed. One of the policemen was draped over the bonnet groaning; the other was lying on the ground not moving.

'Quick!' yelled Craig. 'Kal, go and get Joel or Samson and bring one of the Landies.'

Kal raced off, with Matata following.

Reuben and Craig ran over to the policemen.

Lucy joined them. 'What happened?'

Reuben was talking to the man lying over the bonnet, who was beginning to recover.

'He says it was ole Tisip with his *rungu*,' said Reuben.

'His club?'

'Yes, he hit both of them. They just weren't expecting it.'

'This guy's in a bad way,' said Craig, who was kneeling beside the other policeman. 'I think his skull's fractured. We need to get him to hospital as quickly as possible.'

Samson came running round the side of the house. 'What is it, Craig?'

'Ole Tisip smashed this guy's skull with his *rungu*.'

Samson swore.

'Get your vehicle,' cried Craig, 'and take him to hospital. If they can't treat him in Shinyanga, tell them to call the Flying Doctor in Nairobi.'

Samson ran off.

Ellie was kneeling beside the man, wiping blood away from his face. 'He's really bad,' she said.

'I just hope Samson can get to the hospital in…'

Joel came roaring round the side of the house in the open Land Rover, with Kal sitting beside him, and Matata clinging on in the back.

'We'll go after them,' shouted Craig. 'Reuben, you'd better come with us.'

'Right.' Reuben jumped in beside Matata.

Craig tore the sling off his shoulder, scrambled in beside Kal, and slammed the door.

'Me too!' shouted Lucy. And before anyone realised, she was squeezed in between Reuben and Matata, and Joel was speeding off.

'Lucy!' Mum's frantic cry was lost in the roar of the engine.

'You shouldn't have come,' yelled Craig.

'Too late!'

'Well, just hang on.'

In the distance, they could see a plume of dust where Toad Face's vehicle was speeding away.

'I reckon he's got about a three-minute start,' said Craig.

Joel knew the tracks and could drive fast, and soon they caught glimpses of the Range Rover through the clouds of dust being thrown up behind it. Gradually, the gap between the vehicles lessened. As they drew nearer, they caught up with the dust from the Range Rover that lingered in the air, and Joel had to slow down as they drove into choking clouds. They emerged from one of these to see ole Tisip leaning out of his window shouting back at them and waving his *rungu*.

'We're gaining on them,' said Reuben. 'Keep going, Joel.'

'He's gone the wrong way,' shouted Craig. 'That track leads to a swamp; he'll never get through there.'

The vehicle in front was definitely slowing.

'See,' said Joel, 'no dust. The track is wet.'

'He's stopped!' cried Kal. 'He's trying to turn round.'

They watched as the vehicle half turned, stopped, went forward a bit, and then tried to reverse. They could hear the engine revving and could see mud flying up from its wheels.

'He's stuck!'

'*Tembo*,' murmured Matata.

'What does that…?' Lucy gasped.

An elephant had stepped out from behind a thicket, and was standing no more than twenty paces from the Range Rover. It seemed puzzled by the vehicle and stood watching it. Then with no warning, it tucked its trunk down, flattened its ears and charged. It hit the vehicle a shuddering blow. The doors burst open; Toad Face leapt out of one side, and ole Tisip the other.

'They're getting away!' yelled Lucy.

'Toad Face isn't,' cried Kal.

They watched in horror as Toad Face tried to run off through the swamp, but he was floundering and kept falling over. The elephant ambled after him – its pace seemed almost leisurely.

Toad Face turned and they could see the look of terror on his face as the elephant closed on him.

It reached out its trunk grasped him round the waist, and raised him high in the air. Toad Face screamed, his legs waved, and he hammered on the trunk with his fists, trying to break the crushing grip.

Lucy blocked her ears to shut out those terrible screams.

Then the screams abruptly ceased as Toad Face was slammed into the ground.

It was Lucy's turn to scream.

The elephant picked up the limp body and slammed it down again. Then it placed a foot on the man's chest.

Lucy shut her eyes tight.

The silence was broken only by the call of a plover.

Craig was the first to speak. 'Where's Matata?'

Lucy's eyes flew open. She looked wildly round. 'No!' she cried. 'He was just here, beside me.'

'There!' shouted Kal, pointing. 'He's chasing ole Tisip.'

'That man killed his father,' said Joel. 'See.'

'Where on earth did he find those?' muttered Craig. 'I thought I'd hidden them.'

'His bow and arrow, you mean?' cried Lucy.

Ole Tisip turned and drew back his arm.

'Look out!' yelled Craig.

But Matata was too far away to hear the warning. The *rungu* came whistling through the air. He threw himself to the ground and rolled away just as it sailed past his head.

Now ole Tisip came at Matata with a drawn *simi*.

Those in the vehicle could do nothing except watch in dread.

'Matata, run!' yelled Kal.

But Matata couldn't. He didn't have time to get up, or even notch an arrow into his bow before ole Tisip was upon him, slashing and stabbing with his *simi*. Matata rolled away again, and again, and a third time – each time, just avoiding the razor-sharp blade as he desperately tried to fend off the attack with one of his arrows. Ole Tisip grabbed the arrow and hurled it aside. Matata was now defenceless. Once more, he twisted away.

Ole Tisip hesitated.

Why?

Matata didn't wait to find out. He leaped to his feet and ran. But this time, ole Tisip didn't follow, he staggered and sank to his knees. He stared at his hands and screamed. The screams died in his throat and he sank to the ground. His body twitched and then lay still.

'What happened?' whispered Lucy.

'He cut his hand when he grabbed the arrow,' said Reuben.

'And the poison did the rest,' said Craig.

'Awesome,' breathed Kal.

'I guess the guy had it coming to him,' said Craig.

The plover was still calling.

'Look,' whispered Kal. 'What's Matata doing now?'

They watched, not daring to breathe. Matata was walking towards the elephant.

'That is Moshi,' murmured Joel.

'What?' cried Lucy.

'This is where she stays,' said Joel. 'She has come back from the hills.'

Lucy hardly dared look. 'Matata will be killed,' she whispered, in a strangled voice as she gripped the seat in front of her.

'No,' whispered Craig. 'Watch.'

Matata was now standing in front of the elephant. His hands were held wide, and he was talking to it.

Moshi seemed confused. She made no attempt to charge

Matata, but rocked on her feet, making groaning noises. Then her legs buckled, she fell to the ground, and rolled onto her side with a great sigh.

'*Kufa*,' murmured Joel.

'She's dead,' said Craig.

'Oh no!' cried Lucy. She put her head in her hands, and didn't raise it until a hand was placed on her shoulder.

'Come,' said Craig.

The others were gathered round the dead elephant. Matata was stroking its trunk and talking quietly to it.

'What's he saying?' whispered Lucy.

'He's telling its spirit that it is now at peace.'

'Now what's he doing?' she asked, as Matata broke off a branch of green leaves from a bush and stuffed it into Moshi's mouth, murmuring to her as he did so.

'He is saying: "sleep well, my friend",' said Craig. 'The Maasai have a special relationship with elephants and regard them almost like their own people. The green leaves are to send her on a peaceful journey.'

'That is just so nice.' Lucy too whispered a message to Moshi. Then she sniffed and wiped her hand across her eyes.

Craig smiled. 'Come and see what Joel has found,' he said, leading her closer to the elephant.

Lucy was really nervous but thought if she was going to be a wildlife vet, she would have to get used to such sights. Moshi had seemed huge that time she chased their Land Rover, but close up, she was simply enormous. Joel had scrambled onto her back and was pointing to a mark behind the ear.

'What is it?' asked Lucy.

'It seems to be an old wound,' said Craig, 'but it's still very swollen.'

Joel took his *simi* from his belt and began cutting through the tough skin.

Again, Lucy knew she had to watch. She wasn't afraid of the sight of blood – and there was plenty of that – and it wasn't horrible, as she feared.

Craig and Matata joined Joel, who was now digging into the wound.

'It goes very deep,' called Craig. 'I reckon it's some sort of abscess.'

'Would it explain her behaviour?' asked Lucy.

'Could do.'

'*Aieeh*!' exclaimed Joel. The whole of his arm was inside the wound. He withdrew it, holding something in his hand, which he passed to Craig.

Craig slid down off the elephant and showed Lucy and Kal.

'An arrowhead!' gasped Lucy.

Craig nodded. 'A poacher's arrow. The wood has rotted away, but the head remained, working its way in towards her brain.'

'Poor Moshi,' said Lucy, 'that's awful.'

'Certainly explains why she was bad tempered.'

'How long has that arrow been there?' asked Kal.

'Could be months or even years; there's no knowing.'

'And Moshi has been suffering all that time?' said Lucy.

'I guess when she bashed the Range Rover it dislodged the arrowhead or burst something in the brain, and that's what killed her.'

'I thought you said arrow poison could kill an elephant,' said Kal.

'It would if it was fresh. The poison on that arrow was probably old when the poacher fired it, that's why it didn't kill her at the time.'

'Not like ole Tisip,' said Kal.

'He wasn't quite so lucky,' agreed Craig, looking across at the body.

'You could call it the justice of the bush,' said Reuben.

'For him and Toad Face,' said Kal.

Reuben nodded. 'It's certainly saved the police and the courts some work. But–' He glanced at Craig. '–I think you should find a better hiding place for those arrows.'

Craig grinned. 'Sure.' He looked at his watch. 'We should get back.'

'Are you just going to leave the bodies?' asked Kal.

Reuben thought for a moment. 'There's no room to take them with us and it will soon be dark. Craig and I will come back tomorrow.'

'But what about hyenas and things?' cried Lucy.

'Perhaps the justice of the bush will be completed by the undertakers of the bush,' murmured Reuben.

Craig nodded. 'It's the way of the bush.'

'And Moshi can go on her last journey in peace,' said Lucy.

'Yes, and her body will return to the soil,' said Craig, smiling. 'Time to go.'

CHAPTER 22

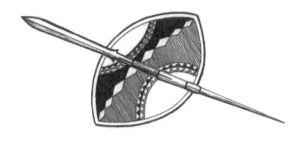

Maasai shield and spear

DAD SPRINGS A SURPRISE

It was dark by the time they got back, but Mum, Dad, Ellie and Diana were anxiously waiting up for them.

'Lucy,' cried Mum, 'you should never have gone off like that! Whatever were you thinking of?'

But Lucy didn't want to talk. She felt so sad about poor Moshi. And seeing Toad Face and ole Tisip, that was really horrible, even if they had got what they deserved.

'Craig!' scolded Diana. 'What were *you* thinking of, taking the children with you?'

'I didn't have much choice; things happened so fast.'

'Well, at least you're all back safely,' said Dad.

'We were so worried,' said Mum.

'We're okay,' said Kal.

'Yes, but there's no knowing what might have…'

'Are the policemen okay?' asked Craig.

'Samson and Onesmo have taken the injured one to Shinyanga,' said Diana, 'and Martha's looking after the other one. He was just bruised. But I still…'

'Mother, I think we all need a drink.'

'I'll get you some tea,' said Ellie.

'I think some of us might need something a bit stronger,' said Craig, his face relaxing into a smile.

∽∂ᅌ∾

The policeman who had been hit in the stomach was fully recovered by the next morning, so immediately after an early breakfast, Craig and Reuben went with him and Joel out to the swamp. But Craig wouldn't let the children go. Lucy was relieved because she didn't want to see poor Moshi again. She waved at their vehicle as it left, then joined the others at the breakfast table.

Dad had just arrived. 'Have you recovered from all your excitement yesterday?' he asked.

Lucy shrugged. She still didn't want to talk about it.

'Your father has some news,' said Mum.

'Oh yes,' said Lucy, not really interested.

'Don't you want to know how he got on at the university?'

'Whatever.'

'Some good news, Lucy,' said Dad.

'What?'

'I'm pleased to say my assessment was correct. Professor Wafula, the head of the department of geology at Nairobi University, was in no doubt as to the quality of the material that I took him.'

Lucy shot up in her seat. 'So everyone's going to be rich!'

'Lucy!' cried Mum.

'Well,' said Diana laughing, 'the government will claim a substantial portion, but it should be an end to our financial worries.'

'Simba is going to be all right, then?' said Kal.

Diana smiled. 'It certainly seems that way.'

'Isn't that splendid news?' said Mum.

'It is just so brilliant!' cried Lucy.

Craig, Reuben, Joel and the policeman returned around noon, towing Toad Face's battered Range Rover, which would be taken to the police pound at Shinyanga.

The policeman confirmed that it was obvious Mr Nagu and ole Tisip – what was left of them – had been involved in an unfortunate accident with an elephant. These things happened in the bush. He would make sure the next of kin were informed.

An hour later, Samson and Onesmo were also back and reported that the policeman with the damaged skull had been stabilised at the hospital in Shinyanga, and that the Flying Doctor service would be taking him to Nairobi for an operation. His life was no longer in danger but he would be in hospital for a number of weeks.

'Poor guy,' said Craig. 'I'm just relieved he's getting the best treatment.'

It was a late lunch for everyone that day.

'So much has happened in the last few days,' said Lucy, helping herself to salad, 'but there are still things I don't understand.'

'Such as?' said Craig.

'Did ole Tisip really kill Matata's dad?'

'Matata certainly thinks he did,' said Kal.

Reuben nodded. 'I think he's right. But all we know for sure is that Punyua, Matata's father, disappeared after some trouble at his *manyatta*.'

'What sort of trouble?'

'Ole Tisip claimed that Punyua's *manyatta* belonged to him and tried to throw him out. I was stationed at Shinyanga at the time, and we were often being called in when there were fights. But ole Tisip was backed by Nagu, and there was nothing we could do. I was furious.'

'So what happened to Punyua?' asked Lucy, sitting down next to Reuben.

'He disappeared.'

'Murdered?'

'We think so,' said Reuben, 'and ole Tisip was the main suspect. But his body was never found – probably dumped in the bush for the hyenas.'

Lucy shuddered. 'The undertakers of the bush,' she murmured.

Reuben nodded. 'So no charges could be brought. Then ole Tisip moved in and took over Punyua's *manyatta*.'

'The Maasai elders with whom we share the ranch were livid, but they couldn't do anything either,' said Craig. 'Punyua was a good man; I knew him, but not well.'

'When Nagu, Toad Face – whatever we call him – had ole Tisip in place,' continued Reuben, 'he used him in laying claim to the Seki Hills.'

'But how did Toad Face find out about the stones?' asked Ellie.

'From one of the Simba board meetings,' said Craig. 'We were discussing ways to solve our funding problems and I told the board that I thought there were valuable minerals in the hills.'

'So when Toad Face heard that Dad was coming, he had to quickly forge the land registration document,' said Ellie.

'That's right,' said Reuben.

'And that's why he wanted Matata, to see if he could get more information from him,' said Kal.

Reuben was nodding.

'And then put men in the hills to stop other people going there,' said Lucy.

'Nagu was very crafty,' said Reuben, 'in everything he did, he made it look as though it was ole Tisip who was organising things: whether it was getting Matata back, laying claim to the hills, or posting guards there.'

'But why did the guards shoot Craig?' asked Mum.

'That was probably a mistake,' said Reuben.

'Well, that's a relief, hey,' said Craig, rubbing his shoulder.

'Sorry, Craig,' said Reuben. 'I think the men panicked when they saw your rifle, shot you, and then didn't know what to do, so they took you to Nagu to let him decide. They probably had an arrangement to meet in the hills.'

'I bet Toad Face got a shock when the men appeared with Mum, Dad and Craig,' said Kal.

'I guess he did, but he hid it pretty well,' said Craig. 'He gave those guys a right pasting and said we would be safe with him.'

'And we were foolish enough to believe him,' said Mum.

Craig nodded. 'By the time we realised he wasn't on our side, it was too late and we were banged up in ole Tisip's *manyatta*.'

'But why did he take us to that dreadful place?' asked Mum.

'That I do know,' said Reuben. 'Nagu imprisoned you there while he went to Shinyanga to get the police and have Craig arrested on those charges he brought up yesterday, but when he got back with the police, you had gone.'

'So he chased after us,' said Kal.

'Yes, with those two policemen,' said Reuben. 'They thought they were going to be killed by the buffaloes. Nagu was yelling and screaming. The men were terrified, and had to overpower him and drag him out of the driving seat.'

'But why did they wait nearly a week before coming back?' asked Diana.

'It took that long before Nagu could get an arrest warrant.'

'So the first time,' said Craig, 'he didn't have a warrant?'

'No, and the police were very reluctant to go with him. But–' Reuben shrugged, '–Nagu could push people around.'

'No longer, thank goodness,' said Diana. She turned to Craig. 'You know, I think we may need to find a new board member.'

Craig insisted on celebrating that evening. He and Samson organised a fire under some massive acacia trees; Kal, Matata, Reuben and the other policeman (whose name was Elijah. Fancy a policeman being called Elijah, thought Lucy) carried down chairs and tables; and Lucy, Ellie and Mum helped Diana and Martha get food ready. Dad kept getting in the way and saying things like: 'You must give me something to do,' and then forgetting what it was. But no one minded.

Lucy remembered the barbecues the family sometimes had at home, when Dad pulled their rickety barbecue on wheels out from under the flowerpots in the garden shed, brushed off the cobwebs, and then couldn't get the charcoal to light because everything was damp. The present setting was what barbecues ought to be like: a warm still night with a beautiful moon, a blazing log fire with its flickering light reflecting off the trees, a yummy smell of roast meat mixed with wood smoke drifting in the air, and the night sounds of Africa all around. She was only sorry that Joel and the cattlemen weren't there because they ought to be sharing in the celebration – and there was a mountain of food.

'What's that noise?' asked Mum.

They could hear a strange grunting sound – and it was coming nearer.

The fire flared, illuminating the edge of the clearing, and there, with his spear and shield, was a Maasai warrior. He was stamping in time to the grunt, crashing his spear against his shield – and advancing towards them.

Fupi growled. Lucy quickly picked her up.

The fire flared again and Lucy saw other warriors following him. The hairs on the back of her neck began to rise. The grunting grew louder, and still the men advanced. Suddenly, she realised: the warrior in the front was Joel! And the one behind was Onesmo; and then the other cattlemen – all in their traditional warrior dress, and all with spears and shields with intricate patterns painted on them. She stood up and cheered.

There was a call from Joel; the men gave a shout and stopped. Everyone clapped. The men laughed, and came and shook everyone by the hand. Craig and Reuben passed round drinks, and the men settled down beside the fire, laughing and chatting.

Lucy thought it was a fantastic evening that only got better. After everyone had eaten, Joel called out to the men and they formed a semi-circle, standing stiff as soldiers. Joel gave a command, and they started bouncing. They kept quite straight and hardly bent their knees, but bounced higher and higher, grunting and nodding their heads in time to the bounce.

'Come on, guys,' called Craig, joining in. 'Sorry, not the girls.'

But Lucy didn't take any notice. She found it really difficult bouncing without bending her knees, and everyone laughed, but she didn't mind. Then Kal and Matata joined them – they were quite good, especially Matata. Craig stopped because his shoulder was hurting but Samson, Reuben and Elijah took his place, and the men cheered even louder. Dad said he wasn't going to make a fool of himself, but Lucy dragged him into the middle. He amazed everyone by being nearly as good as Onesmo. 'It's all that climbing up and down hills I do,' said Dad, embarrassed.

One of the men called out and everyone stopped. Reuben was pushed into the middle, the men started grunting again, and Reuben had to bounce on his own. He winked at Kal, and really started to bounce. Everyone was grunting now and clapping. Even Fupi joined in, barking in time to the bounce. Lucy couldn't believe how high Reuben went – like he was on the moon.

Reuben grinned and stopped. He was hardly breathing.

'What's this?' cried Kal, picking up something from the ground. 'It fell out of your pocket, Reuben.'

'Oh no!' cried Reuben. 'I'm so sorry. Samson collected the post when he was in Shinyanga and asked me to pass this letter on.'

'Who's it for?' asked Lucy.

'It's addressed to Professor Bartlett.'

'Me?' exclaimed Dad. 'But I'm not a professor.' He looked mystified as he took the letter from Reuben and opened it. 'Good Lord!'

'Who's it from?' asked Kal.

'It's a letter from the Dean of Science at the University of Nairobi.'

'Why's he written to you?'

'Well, I'm blowed!' Dad looked round the gathering, beaming. 'He's offered me a temporary chair at the university while Professor Wafula goes on a period of study leave to the United States.'

'What's that mean?' said Lucy.

'It means Dad is going to be a professor,' said Ellie.

'A professor!'

'Hmm, Professor Bartlett,' said Dad. 'I rather like the sound of that.'

'That's fantastic, Dad,' cried Ellie. She and Lucy rushed up and hugged him.

'Cool, Dad,' said Kal.

'Will you accept?' asked Craig.

Dad thought for a moment. 'You know, I think I will. Professor Bartlett, eh?'

'Does that mean we have to go and live in Kenya?' asked Ellie.

'Your mother and I will have to talk about it,' said Dad, 'but it's more likely she will stay with you while you are in school in England, and bring you out during the holidays.'

'You must come and stay at Simba,' said Craig.

'What, come out here for school holidays?' cried Ellie.

'Why not?'

'Craig, do you really mean that?' asked Mum.

'Of course. I insist.'

'That is mega awesome,' murmured Kal, shaking his head in disbelief.

'Wow!' breathed Lucy. She picked up Fupi and hugged her.

If you enjoyed *The Ant-Lion*, watch out for the next African Safari Adventure:

The Elephant-Shrew

Lucy, Kal, Ellie, Matata, and of course Fupi, in helping to move a rare but dangerous antelope from the coast of Tanzania to Simba wildlife ranch, are thrown into further hair-raising adventures by the discovery of an ancient map, messages scratched on cave walls, and hidden ruins in the forest, all of which speak of a terrible bygone culture.

But has that time really passed?

Why does Matata find the ruins so scary?

What happens in the under-water cave of the rock-cod?

Who is the mysterious old man who never talks?

And is the elephant-shrew quite what it seems?

Don't buy this book if you are afraid of eagles.

THE SERIES

Everyone who goes to East Africa hopes to see the Big Five: lion, elephant, buffalo, leopard and rhinoceros, but very few are aware of the Little Five, from which the
AFRICAN SAFARI ADVENTURES
take their titles.

If you are lucky enough to be taken on safari, watch out for the Little Five.

The ANT-LION is an insect, the adult of which flies at night. It looks like a damselfly or small dragonfly.

The ELEPHANT-SHREW. Several species occur in East Africa, most of which are the size of large mice. One that occurs in coastal forests is the size of a small dog.

The BUFFALO-WEAVER is a black bird with a red beak, similar in size to a thrush. It nests in colonies, building an untidy nest of sticks.

The LEOPARD-TORTOISE is the most likely of the Little Five to be noticed. It occurs in dry bush and can be recognised by the black blotches on its sandy-coloured shell.

The RHINOCEROS-BEETLE is one of the largest beetles in Africa. Only the male has the large "horn" from which this insect gets its name.